A K-9 MOUNTAIN PROMISE

HELENA SMRCEK

MIX
Paper | Supporting responsible forestry
FSC® C021394
www.fsc.org

LOVE INSPIRED®
INSPIRATIONAL ROMANCE

Recycling programs for this product may not exist in your area.

ISBN-13: 978-1-335-62169-6

A K-9 Mountain Promise

Love Inspired
22 Adelaide St. West, 41st Floor
Toronto, Ontario M5H 4E3, Canada
www.LoveInspired.com

HarperCollins Publishers
Macken House, 39/40 Mayor Street Upper,
Dublin 1, D01 C9W8, Ireland
www.HarperCollins.com

Printed in Lithuania

1 2 3 4 5 6 7 8 9 10 LIT 28 27 26 25

There he was, standing right in front of her.

"I was just about to knock."

"Saved you the effort," she said. The front door shut behind her with a resolute thud. Abby looked around the front yard. "Where is Charlotte?"

"Over there." Noah strode toward the detached garages. "Look." He motioned toward the side yard.

Charlotte stood there, a yellow Frisbee in her hand, two eager Vizslas watching her every move.

"You have to sit first, Briggs. I'll throw the Frisbee, but only if you listen."

Briggs sat next to Rosie.

She smiled. "Ready?" With a flick of her wrist, the Frisbee sailed through the air. The dogs took off running. Briggs got it first, then ran a few circles around Rosie, who tried to snatch it out of his mouth. Charlotte laughed.

It filled Abby with joy when she heard the sweet sound of her daughter laughing.

"Thank you, Noah," she said softly.

"For what?"

"I haven't seen her this happy in months." Looking at him, her breath caught.

No. Absolutely not. She wouldn't go there. She couldn't.

Could she?

Helena Smrcek, an award-winning author, writes heartfelt romances filled with second chances and the promise of lasting love. Her passion for storytelling began as a teen freelancer for Mississauga News and blossomed into a lifelong journey of weaving tales that touch the heart. When not writing, Helena enjoys audiobooks, farm life and traveling in search of fresh inspiration. She lives on a farm in Southern Ontario with her husband, three rambunctious Vizslas, four cats, three goats and an undisclosed number of chickens.

Books by Helena Smrcek

Love Inspired

A K-9 Mountain Promise

Visit the Author Profile page at LoveInspired.com.

Beloved, let us love one another:
for love is of God; and every one that
loveth is born of God, and knoweth God.
—*1 John 4:7*

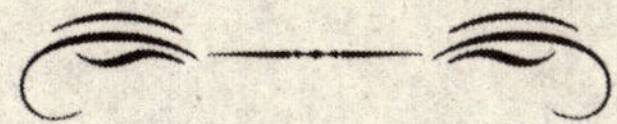

For Martin, my husband, steadfast supporter and lifelong partner in every adventure—thank you for sharing this journey and every chapter of life with me.

Chapter One

As the rugged beauty of Colorado unfolded before them, Abby Clifford's heart filled with both trepidation and hope. She whispered silent prayers for a future where laughter would rule and where her daughter Charlotte's smile would shine brightly once again.

Everything seemed to be changing at lightning speed. She'd never dreamed that she could feel this old at thirty-one. Abby tucked a strand of her blond hair behind her ear. This short bob was a spur-of-the-moment decision, and it drove her crazy. If only she'd asked her stylist to leave it long enough for a ponytail. Abby caught a glimpse of her pink manicured fingernails. The white band on her finger reminded her of the absent five-carat wedding ring. *God, please stop the disappointment and pain.*

A popular country singer's voice filled the car for the fourth time as her playlist started again. Abby exhaled, praying this trip would end. Soon.

"Are we there yet?" Her six-year-old daughter's silver-bell voice interrupted her thoughts as Abby turned off the main road and passed through the familiar open gate. She drove up a gravel driveway she knew well. The log house looked as welcoming as ever, and so did the coach house to the right.

"Yes, we're here, sweetheart." Abby reached toward the back seat and rested her hand on Charlotte's knee. Her daughter had done so well, keeping herself busy with the contents of her

     A K-9 Mountain Promise

travel box of activities they had put together for this journey. A smile flittered across Abby's lips when she recalled Charlotte's excitement while spending her twenty-dollar bill at the bargain store, filling her basket with crayons, coloring books, stickers and little craft kits. The only rule she had to follow was no candy and no glitter. Abby reached toward the back seat and rested her hand on Charlotte's knee.

"You have been such a good girl." The words caught in her throat. This road trip was the longest they had ever taken together. And even though the road led straight west from their home in the suburbs of St. Louis, Abby had driven it only once before. The week of her parents' funeral.

"You've been such a good sport." The twelve-hour drive from St. Louis had been exhausting, especially for her six-year-old daughter, who didn't really understand what this road trip was—an exodus from everything she had known so far. Scattered rays of the setting sun filtered in through the branches as the sky darkened above the mountains in the distance. Only a few more minutes, they could get out of this car, have a quick supper and rest. Abby hoped that Charlotte's first visit to the old log house, the home of the grandparents she'd never met, would be a good one.

"Is this where we're staying tonight?" Charlotte's mouth gaped open. "In a house made of trees?"

"Yes," Abby said. As exhaustion set in, all she really wanted was a good night's sleep. The sunrise would bring another day, one filled with fresh ideas and possibly a smile or two. She glanced at her daughter. Her pink shirt had a little ice-cream stain on the front, and there was a green sprinkle stuck to the end of one of her golden braids. She missed her bubbling laughter. Would it ever come back?

This was the first time the two of them had done something this adventurous without Ken. Abby's now ex-husband had made it abundantly clear that his new wife—and their baby due to arrive the next month—took absolute priority. Abby silently shook her head. No matter what life brought her way, Charlotte would come first, always.

Abby looked up the winding driveway and relaxed the tight grip on her steering wheel. She glanced at her girl, who seemed to shrink into a protective shell. How could she encourage her daughter's keen desire to explore and learn new things when she was in so much pain? This new Charlotte, visibly suffering from the divorce, made Abby anxious.

Lord, please let this be a good decision. We need a fresh start.

Abby forced her thoughts back to the present. The driveway opened onto a clearing, and she pulled up to the garage door. Hopefully, they'd make it inside before the downpour. The car came to a halt in the familiar spot where her dad used to park his red Ford pickup. Abby shut off the engine and let out a long sigh. They were here. This was their new start, far away from her city friends and all that she had known for the past decade.

Her eyes rested on the towering mountains surrounding the log house her parents had built years ago. It was hers now— it had been for the past decade—but this was the first time she had come back, since their funeral. A wave of sadness swept over her. Abby was an only child, with no relatives in this town. She'd not stayed in touch with any high school or church friends and doubted anyone would remember her. She and Charlotte would be utterly alone up on this mountain. What had she been thinking? But what other options did she have? This log home and the detached garage with a small loft apartment above were the only assets left to her in the settlement. Ken had taken the rest.

Ten years of marriage down the drain. She pinched the bridge of her nose. They'd been divorced for a year now, yet every thought of him felt like a dagger in her heart. The sale of their family home took a little longer than expected, giving Abby time to get a part-time job at a local coffee shop, while Charlotte was at preschool. The closing of the sale of their house brought an end to that too. Abby and Charlotte had to move, and the only place for her to go was Hope Rock, Colorado. Now she was on her own.

"Can I get out of the car, Mommy?" Abby smiled because she had her daughter. And she would make it her life's mission to make sure no one else ever hurt her baby.

"Yes, of course." Abby loosened her clenched jaw.

The interior light of her car came on as Charlotte opened the door. Abby pulled at the door handle as the garage door started to roll up. Her eyebrows knitted. She stepped out of the car and adjusted her white athleisure outfit. The wind picked up, sending shivers down her arms. How had she forgotten that this place was cold, even in August?

"Charlotte," she called out to her daughter. According to their agreement, her tenant, and high school boyfriend, Noah Ross, should have moved out days ago. Abby reached for Charlotte's hand and instinctively drew her closer. What was the red pickup truck parked in front of the stairs to the apartment over the garage doing here?

"Maybe you should get back into the car," she whispered, not wanting to scare her. She'd barely finished her sentence when two medium-size brown dogs sprinted out of the garage and circled around them. With tails wagging, they jumped up and licked their faces. Charlotte giggled. Squealing with joy, Charlotte climbed back into the car and quickly shut the door. The dogs stood up on their hind legs and licked the car window. Charlotte laughed.

Suddenly, a male voice boomed from the garage. "Briggs! Rosie! Heel!" The commotion ceased as fast as it had begun. Abby looked up. A man in a plaid shirt, worn jeans and a fawn-colored Stetson walked toward her, boxes in his arms.

Noah Ross?

What was he doing here?

Without hesitation, the man set the boxes down in the bed of his pickup and stepped forward. Still a head taller than her, his frame had filled in, as the teenage boy she'd loved grew into a man. Her former boyfriend was even more handsome than she remembered. She cleared her throat. A lot had changed in twelve years.

"Hi, welcome," he said, as if they were the best of friends. He still used the same woodsy aftershave. When his brown eyes locked with hers, a bitter memory brought her back to reality. This was Noah, the first man who had ever betrayed her.

She cleared her throat.

"Hey." Abby took two steps back. "I didn't expect to see you here," she said, trying to sound casual. He seemed taller than she remembered. His hair was still chestnut brown, and the very same curl she liked to brush off his forehead hung loosely above his left eyebrow.

Charlotte peered at the stranger through the passenger window. The two dogs sat patiently by the door, excited grins on their faces.

"Sorry to surprise you like this." His brown eyes smiled at her. "I was just making sure the heat is on in the house."

That smile used to make her weak in the knees. But that was a lifetime ago.

"Thank you."

"No problem. Glad you made it before the storm. I left a few groceries in the kitchen for you."

"Thanks, but you really didn't need to do that."

"Here are the keys." He reached into the pocket of his well-worn jeans.

Their fingers touched as she accepted the familiar bunch.

Noah hesitated, as if unsure of what to do next. He cleared his throat. "If you don't mind me asking, what are your plans for this place?"

"We'll stay for the rest of the summer and freshen the house up a bit. When Charlotte goes back to school in the fall, we'll move to town, and I can run this as an Airbnb."

She also needed to find a job, but that wasn't any of his business.

"An Airbnb?"

Did she hear a hint of disappointment in his voice?

"Maybe. I need to take things one day at a time." Abby pocketed the keys.

"Sure. And who is this?" His tone instantly lightened as he smiled at the girl staring at them through the window.

"This is my daughter, Charlotte."

Charlotte looked up at Noah.

"Can I come out now?" Her voice was muffled through the closed door.

"Yes, yes, of course," Abby responded.

As soon as her pink Crocs touched the driveway, the dogs were ready to play. Charlotte laughed.

"What kind are they?"

"Rosie. Briggs. Sit," Noah ordered his dogs. "Hungarian Vizslas. They're good at hunting birds, but their favorite thing is snuggling on the sofa and watching TV. Do you like to watch cartoons?"

Charlotte nodded. Her blue eyes locked on the dog with the pink collar, which had a glittering heart-shaped pendant dangling from it.

"Can I pet them?"

"No." Abby cut the conversation off before Noah could respond.

When her daughter froze, Abby bit her lip. That was too harsh. What was the harm in letting her pet his dogs?

"Sorry. Of course, you can pet them if it's okay with Noah."

"Sure thing," he said, his beaming smile at full force.

Briggs and Rosie wiggled their tails, then licked Charlotte's hands, clearly enjoying her attention.

"Here." Noah passed her a tennis ball. "They're good at fetch."

"Be careful," Abby said as Charlotte tossed the ball and watched the two dogs chase after it.

"I'm not scared of them, Mommy." Charlotte accepted the ball straight from Rosie's mouth and ran to her.

"Thank you for all your help," Abby reached for her daughter's licked hand. "But it's been a long drive. We're exhausted."

"Of course." He reached into his pocket and pulled out a fob to remotely start his truck.

The rumble of an engine made Abby turn around. How had she not noticed the bright red F-150 parked inside the coach house garage? It looked so much like the one her dad used to drive. She swallowed the lump in her throat. Maybe this was a bad idea.

"Briggs, Rosie. Come." Noah patted his thigh.

"Thanks again for stopping by," she called after him.

"No problem. Didn't want you to come back to a cold house." He turned around and held her gaze momentarily, as if he could still read her. And then, without another word, he strode toward his truck. She glimpsed his worn cowboy boots and silently wondered if those were still the same pair she had given him for his eighteenth birthday.

"I like Rosie the best. Briggs is a friendly dog, too. Are you and Noah friends?" Charlotte looked up, her eyes full of questions.

"We used to be. When we were kids, but that was a long time ago."

She stood in the driveway, holding her daughter's hand, as he opened the truck's back door and let his dogs in. When Noah hoisted himself up into the seat of that red truck, she pursed her lips.

Used to be.

He drove slowly toward them, then rolled down the window.

"Hey, text me if you need anything in town." He waved his hand and headed down the driveway. Her heart did a little jump.

How could things be so different yet feel the same? She held on to Charlotte a bit tighter. No, all of *that* had been gone for a long time. This was their time to heal and rebuild their lives. She glanced toward the driveway, but Noah's truck was already gone. Thunder rumbled over their heads, and the first drops of heavy rain hit the ground as Abby grabbed two large bags from the back seats and herded Charlotte toward the open garage.

As Noah drove down what had been his driveway for the past ten years, a country tune filled the cab. He reached behind him and petted his two faithful companions, sitting on the crew bench.

"So, that was Abby, just in case you were wondering. And the little one's name is Charlotte." He stopped, flicked on a blinker and turned onto the main road. "How long do you think they will stay?" He continued the one-sided conversation—his dogs were always attentive listeners. "Come fall, Charlotte will need to find a school. Abby said she wants to move to town. I don't blame her. The driveway is a pain to plow in the winter. She'll need a pickup if she wants to stay there."

A soft whine reminded him that as much as Briggs was keen on listening, he was even keener on the dog treats Noah kept in the middle console.

"All right, since you behaved so well. For a Vizsla, anyway." He opened the compartment, reached in and offered them two treats. They instantly disappeared. Rosie stuck her paw between the front seats and rested it on the console.

"No. That's all. Now sit, or I'll pull over and put you in a harness. We've got to be careful, especially in your condition."

Rosie retracted her paw and settled down. Briggs nestled next to her just as the windshield wipers came to life.

"Here comes the rain. Hope the girls managed to unpack the car."

If only she would let him help. Abby hadn't wanted to chat; that much he could tell. But there was so much he wanted to say to her.

God, I'm not asking You to turn back time, but please show me how to be a good friend to both of them.

Noah passed the road sign that said, Welcome to Hope Rock, just as a thunderclap boomed. He turned right at the gas station and pulled into a parking spot next to a low-rise building. This was still new to him. He'd never lived in a condo. He would have to remember to tell Abby that he wasn't completely moved out yet. Some of his stuff was still in the loft above the coach house garage. Finding a self-storage unit had proved to be more difficult than expected.

The other problem was his dogs. They were rightfully confused by the lack of space and their inability to dart outside and run free around the lake behind the log house.

"Let's get you home. I've got to be at work in half an hour." He opened the back door and clicked on their leashes. Rosie hesitated. She didn't love the rain. But after Briggs jumped out, she decided to follow. They obediently walked along the path to the back of the building. Noah missed the forest behind the cabin, for there was nowhere to walk his dogs here. Perhaps he could ask Abby if she would let him bring them up to the cabin a couple of times a week for a walk.

Noah opened the back entrance to the building with his key. He kept the dogs close to him, wrapping their leashes around his wrist. Thankfully, they learned fast and were no longer pulling. Noah looked up the stairs leading to his condo and halted. The sterile smell of disinfectant left much to be desired; how he missed the fresh mountain air.

The super was on the landing, hands on her hips. Her baggy shirt sported a few stains. She waved a broom in Noah's direction. Briggs and Rosie somehow understood that this person wouldn't pet them anytime soon and hid behind Noah.

"If you think you can fool me by using the back door, then you're mistaken, Dr. Ross. It's in the bylaws of this building. No pets allowed. You can take them to your clinic or find a kennel, but you can't keep them here."

"Brenda, you know they are good and don't bark. I don't understand why that's such an issue."

"Rules are rules. And how many times do I need to tell you not to let them do their business on my grass?"

"*Your* grass?"

"You know what I mean. Just think, what would this place look like if everyone did as they pleased?"

"I'll sort this out with my realtor and lawyer. The contract I signed doesn't say that I'm not allowed to have dogs in my condo." He took out his keys. "If you would excuse me, I need to get ready for work."

"You better make sure their wet paws don't mess the stairs. I just mopped."

"Sorry about that. The rain just started."

Brenda frowned. Her glare darkened. "You're off to work, right? Are you taking them with you?"

"I don't see how that's any of your concern."

"If they stay here while you're not at home, I'll call the humane society and have them removed." Then she turned around and walked to her apartment.

Noah patted his leg.

"Let's go." The three of them went up toward his place, only to find a yellow note stuck to the door. Brenda was very determined to uphold law and order. He would have left had he been renting this place. But since the condo was his, things were complicated. Noah shook his head. Was it possible that the woman was correct and by some mistake his realtor had omitted the fact that this building didn't allow pets?

He let the dogs inside his apartment, shut the door behind them and crumpled up the sticky note. Noah surveyed the boxes piled around the place.

Even the old loft above the garage would be better than this concrete block. Yes, it would lack the new-paint smell, but it was bigger and brighter than this cramped apartment. He'd loved living there while Abby's parents were still alive. After their deaths, he'd decided that renting the log house would be a better option for him, the dogs and Abby. He had taken care of the place as if it were his own, hoping that one day she would return to Hope Rock.

Noah glanced out the window. He missed the log cabin. And all the items that reminded him of years gone by. The starkness of his new place grated on his soul. Most of all, he missed the magnificent views of the lake that used to make him smile every morning.

"We'll just have to get used to this place, I guess." Rosie nuzzled her head into his empty hand. "You're such a good girl." He gave her a little rub under her chin. Briggs eagerly stuck out his nose, unwilling to miss out. "Of course, you're a good boy, too. But I've got to get ready for work. Sorry, pups."

He pulled a pair of clean scrubs out of a box. They could use an ironing, but unfortunately, he didn't know where it was in all the boxes.

He wondered, would Abby be able to maintain the log house while taking care of her daughter? The drive to school alone would take a couple of hours out of her day, especially in the winter.

He would have to text her to ask when would be a good time to stop by and pick up the last of his stuff.

Noah ran his hands through his hair in the bathroom mirror. Thankfully, there were no strands of gray in his unruly chestnut-brown mop. He quietly scoffed at his reflection. He had done everything he set out to do—earned his doctor of veterinary medicine, gotten a job in his hometown, saved up enough money to buy his own place and bred and trained emotional support dogs—a dream come true. So why did his life feel so empty?

He refreshed the dogs' water, added a couple of scoops of kibble to their bowls and patted their heads. Their brown eyes followed him to the door. These two were amazing companions, yet he definitely missed that special someone in his life.

"Rosie, you're in charge, so don't let him go through my boxes and chew up things." His sweet female dog looked at him as if committing his instructions to memory. "And you, Briggs, guard the house. If Brenda tries to get in, bark, but don't bite her." Briggs looked a little concerned. "Don't worry, buddy," Noah scratched his ears. "She won't come in. For that, she would need a court order, and the wheels in this town don't move that fast. I promise I'll figure this out."

He grabbed his keys and locked the door behind him. Indeed, he had a lot of stuff to figure out.

Noah rushed down the stairs, hoping Brenda was no longer patrolling the hallways. If he were honest with himself, he would have to admit that the night shifts seemed to be getting longer and the emptiness of his life heavier. He loved being a veterinarian, and working nights came with the territory of being the only emergency clinic within a 20-mile radius. During the past two years of his practice, the Hope Rock Veterinary Clinic, he'd gotten to know most of the pets in the area. He loved his job, yet all the cuddly critters failed to fill that empty space in his heart. He longed for someone to share his life with—and seeing Abby today made him even more aware of the ever-present loneliness.

On his way to the clinic, he stopped at a drive-through for a burger, since the vending machine in the waiting room of the clinic was full of salty and sugary snacks. They would do in a pinch, but there was a limit to how many chocolate bars you could eat for dinner.

With the windshield wipers swishing, a lonely country tune played on the radio as he drove through the pouring rain. The melancholy mood made him ponder how much things had changed since that fateful night.

Chapter Two

As the garage door closed, Abby and Charlotte entered the house. The familiar creak welcomed her as they stepped over the threshold. How many times had she rushed out of this door, her mother calling after her not to forget her lunch?

"I promise, this will be fun," she said to Charlotte, trying to sound enthusiastic.

"Is this the man's house?" Her daughter's eyes scanned the space. A worry wrinkle appeared on her forehead.

"No, sweetie. It's ours."

"But our home is in the city."

Abby slipped off her shoes. "I explained all that, didn't I?"

"But you didn't say our new house will be brown." She crossed her arms over her chest. "I don't like brown. And it smells funny."

This was not a good time to get into an argument with her daughter.

"We can open the windows and air things out." She was right. The house smelled a little stale. "But why don't I show you the kitchen first? Noah said he bought some groceries for us. Let's see what we can make for dinner."

"I don't want to make dinner," she whined.

"Okay."

"It's not okay. I want Daddy." Charlotte started to cry.

Abby blew out a long breath. Moments like this made her hate her ex even more. He'd just left, as if she and their daughter no longer mattered, and built a new life with someone else. Great.

"I'm going to take my bag to the bedroom and then make supper. You can explore the house. I'll call you when the food is ready."

"I don't want to explore this ugly brown house," Charlotte wailed.

Abby's heart was breaking for her daughter. The color of the log house wasn't their biggest problem right now. But how could she explain this to her?

"Would you like a hug?"

"No." Charlotte dropped to the floor, curled up into a tight ball and wrapped her arms around her knees. "I want my daddy."

"Sweetheart." Abby knelt next to the sobbing child and gently pulled her closer, struggling to hold back her own tears. She wanted her old life back, too, but Abby didn't have the luxury of crying over all that was lost right now. Her daughter didn't need to see her tears. There would be plenty of time for that after she tucked her into bed.

"Charlotte," she whispered when the deep sobs subsided. "I know that you miss Daddy. I miss him, too. But you and I will—" She took a deep breath. Then continued. "We'll check out this house and see if we can make it pretty."

Charlotte gave her a slight nod.

"Can I have a dog?"

"What?"

Her daughter's teary eyes met hers. "It'd make me feel better. I know it."

"But honey, we just got here. We need to—"

"I really like Rosie." Charlotte tried to smile through her tears. "She's a very pretty girl dog."

Abby got up, staring at her daughter. There was no way they

could get a dog at that moment, but she would explain that to Charlotte tomorrow, after they'd both had a good night's sleep.

"Tell you what. Why don't we pretend this is a camping trip? We can talk about a dog tomorrow."

Charlotte sprang to her feet and wrapped her arms around Abby's waist.

"Thank you, Mommy. You're the best."

"Hold on." Abby reached for the tear-streaked face. "Just to be clear, I'm not agreeing to a dog."

Charlotte grinned. "Where's my room?"

"Through the kitchen, to the hallway. First room on the right."

What had just happened? Abby ran her fingers through her hair. One thing was for sure. No dog would move into this house anytime soon.

Her bag in hand, she strode toward the kitchen. The old wallpaper was still hanging, and so were the curtains Mom had made decades ago. And then she noticed the large box on the island. What had Noah been thinking? Abby set her bag on the barn-board dining room table. Then she reached for the card tucked into the box.

Welcome home.

This hadn't been her home for over twelve years, and coming back to this cabin was difficult, to say the least. She tossed the card onto the counter and looked inside the box. As kind as this gesture was, Abby felt a tinge of disappointment. It was all dry goods. It would take at least an hour to make a meal from any of this.

Abby walked over and opened the fridge. At least this appliance wasn't twenty years old. There were milk, eggs, butter, cold cuts and cheese on the shelves.

Noah, how will I ever repay you for this?

She had to admit that this haul of groceries was one of the kindest things anyone had done for her in a long while. The familiar lump formed in her throat. She was determined not to give in to the grief. This was their new start.

"How about a grilled cheese sandwich for supper?" Abby called out.

"With ketchup?" Charlotte ran into the kitchen.

"Let me see." Abby checked the box on the counter. "Yes, we've got ketchup."

"Yay!" Charlotte clapped.

"How do you like your room?"

"I don't. It's scary. Can I help make dinner?" Charlotte reached for the loaf of bread.

"Sure. But first, let's wash our hands. The bathroom is this way."

They stepped into the tight space, which contained a single vanity, toilet and bathtub. Rust stains circled the drain. Forest-themed wallpaper surrounded them.

"It smells funny." Charlotte wrinkled her nose.

Abby turned on the tap. "We can fix that tomorrow, too. Here." She passed her a bar of soap.

"I want my sparkly soap," Charlotte said.

"Let's make do with what we have right now, sweetie." She didn't have the heart to tell her that the closest store selling her favorite pink cotton candy–smelling soap was at least an hour away. "We'll make our grilled cheese, and then we can change into pj's and watch a show on your iPad."

Charlotte nodded, drying her hands, then skipped toward the kitchen.

"Come on, Mama," Charlotte called. "I found a frying pan."

Abby headed to the kitchen, took the pan from her daughter and set it on the stove. "One thing, honey. This is a gas stove. I don't want you to turn it on without me. Ever." Abby twisted the knob. A blue flame sprang to life.

Charlotte's eyes grew wide.

"This is real fire. So, no silly stuff, you hear me?"

"Yes, Mom."

"You don't need to be scared of it, just remember to be careful." Abby tried to reassure her while silently wondering where she could buy the things necessary for childproofing the house.

Sitting at the old wooden table, grilled cheese sandwiches smothered with ketchup on the plates, Abby poured milk into their glasses.

"Mom, why did Mr. Noah get the groceries for us?" Charlotte asked as she took a bite. Ketchup smeared across her face. "And how did he know cheddar cheese is my favorite?"

"Well, he probably thought we would get here late and we would be hungry."

He had also known that cheddar had always been Abby's favorite, but if she mentioned that, it would unleash an avalanche of questions. She wasn't quite ready for that.

"And it was nice of him to do that, don't you think so?"

"And I liked his dogs. Do you think they'll come back to visit us sometimes?"

The last thing she needed was Charlotte bonding with Noah or his dogs. For now, she had no plan past this summer.

"How about you go put on your pajamas? Then we'll watch one of your shows."

"Can I pick?"

"Of course." Abby dropped their plates into the sink—she'd deal with dirty dishes later.

Picking up her bag, still sitting on the dining room table, Abby walked into her parents' former bedroom. It had been hers since the terrible car accident ten years ago, much like the rest of this log house—yet she had never slept in this room, nor this cabin, after their untimely deaths. A pang squeezed her chest as her eyes took in the familiar space. Nothing had changed. Her pictures, documenting the life she left behind all those years ago, lined the wall opposite the king-size bed. She had been so happy then.

Her bag landed on the bed with a muffled thud. She opened it and rummaged for her pajamas.

She pulled back the comforter. The sheets smelled fresh. A frown creased her forehead. Noah's doing?

"Mom?"

Abby looked up. The sight of her daughter in her pajamas brought a smile to her face. They were most likely the only pink thing in this entire house—a reminder of how much their lives had changed.

"Can I sleep with you in your bed tonight?" the little silver-bell voice asked.

"Of course, sweetheart. Get your iPad while I get ready." She tousled her daughter's hair and made quick strides toward the bathroom, unwilling to let Charlotte see the tears filling her eyes.

Noah parked his truck in the spot behind the vet clinic clearly marked with his name. He'd tried to explain to the clinic's receptionist, Cindy Bower, that it was unnecessary. Still, she argued that all the veterinarians needed a designated parking spot in case of an emergency. He let Cindy have her way.

"Dr. Noah," she said with mild panic in her voice as soon as he stepped through the door. "Come quick." Cindy rushed toward the examination room, her cat-print scrubs swishing.

He dropped his takeout on the reception desk and followed her.

"A hiker brought this in a few minutes ago. I was hoping that you wouldn't be late. Dr. Gina had already left, because there were no more appointments, and I don't know what to do with this." She pointed to a cardboard box sitting under a heat lamp.

The alarm in her voice set Noah's adrenaline coursing. Cindy had worked at the clinic for two years now, and the mother of three usually kept a calm demeanor. She was particularly levelheaded during emergencies, which he always appreciated.

"What is it?" He stepped closer to the heat lamp and peered into the box. His breath caught.

"I don't know. It's too small to tell." She pursed her lips.

"Let me see."

"Is it a coyote pup?"

"No, it's a domestic dog. I can't tell the breed, but it's definitely not a coyote." Her eyes grew wide. "A puppy? Left alone in a forest?"

Noah put on a pair of latex gloves. The little critter seemed to be asleep. "Have you given it any water?"

"I wouldn't know how."

"Pass me a dropper, please."

As Cindy rushed to find one, Noah carefully lowered his fingers into the box, not wanting to startle the pup. It didn't.

She handed him the dropper filled with water.

Noah gently lifted the puppy out. "Let's take a look at you." The little dog didn't squirm, nor did it open its eyes.

"Can you save it?"

"It's a male, please mark it on his chart. He's really young," Noah said under his breath. "I'll try my best. But this little one has been left alone for a while."

Noah lifted the puppy's head and examined it. He gently opened his mouth. "Let's try this." He squeezed the dropper. The water ran down the furry chin. "Okay, you've got to help us here, buddy." Noah tried again. This time, as if the pup understood, it moved his tongue. Noah repeated the process. The little puppy struggled to lift his head as he sniffed around for his mom's milk.

"That's encouraging."

The vet carefully laid the tiny dog on the examination table. He gently lifted each small paw to ensure no bones were broken. Then Noah examined the abdomen. "He is fine. Now we have to figure out how to get him hydrated and then try to feed the little critter."

"So, what do we do?"

"First, let me run an IV line to give him some fluids. Then we need to figure out how we are going to feed him."

"I don't mind staying and feeding the puppy." Her smile beamed. "The girls have youth group tonight. Dave can drive them."

"Thanks, Cindy. Are there any appointments booked for this evening?"

"You should have a quiet night, for a Monday. There's only one appointment scheduled, Mrs. Sweetwater. She's bringing Toby. He's not eating well. That's it, unless there are more emergencies. We have three cats and one dog in for overnight observation. I've set up their food on the counter in the kennel room. They all have fresh water, and the litter boxes are clean. Bowser will need a walk around nine."

"Thanks." Noah scooped up the little puppy and placed it back in the box. "You didn't need to do that. I can manage."

"Just say the word and I'll stay to help." Cindy turned around and walked back to her desk. "Would you like me to put your dinner in the staff room fridge?" she called out.

"Don't worry about that." Noah adjusted the heat lamp. He opened the supply drawer and took out all that would be needed to rehydrate the small dog. Now that the most urgent step was done, and the IV drip was firmly taped to the pup's front paw, Noah petted the tired animal with his index finger. Was it even possible to save it?

"If you don't need anything else..." Cindy leaned against the door frame.

Noah looked up.

"Then I'll head out." Her warm smile lit up her face.

"Sure. And thank you."

"No worries." She adjusted the strap of her purse. "Call me if you need anything." She glanced at the box with the dog.

"I appreciate that. Have a great evening, Cindy."

"Your food is in the fridge," she said, then headed for the front door. But just as she pulled at the door handle, Cindy glanced over her shoulder, then took a step back. "What are you going to feed it?"

Noah tapped his index finger against his cheek. "What can we make you for supper, buddy?" He spoke in a soothing voice while his mind raced. He needed to save this little pup. After all, saving critters, big and small, was what he did. Cindy returned to the examination room.

"Any ideas?" she asked.

"Well, I was thinking the simplest thing would be the kitten milk substitute we store for emergencies. It'll have to do for tonight."

"Why didn't I think of that right away? I'll place a bottle in the warmer." Cindy rushed out the door.

He felt a twinge of guilt. Her family was most likely ready for the Wednesday night church activities, waiting for her to get home so they could all go together. Cindy and Dave had been married for seventeen years, and their daughters had attended his Sunday school class before they graduated to the youth group. Would he ever have a family of his own?

The puppy squirmed, tilted his head.

"Looking for some food? Now that's a good sign. Give us a moment."

As if on cue, Cindy rushed in, holding a small feeding bottle.

"Here you go, hope it works. So, if you don't think you'll need me, I have to run, so we can take only one car to the church."

"Thank you."

She smiled and rushed out the door.

A feeling of loneliness suddenly swept over him. Noah had his dogs and a Sunday school class full of kids. He thought of the log house. Abby and Charlotte were most likely getting ready for bed. He had to smile, recalling the little girl running around with Rosie and Briggs. His heart swelled with an unexpected feeling of—what?

He had seen firsthand what kind of grief a broken marriage caused. Charlotte's eyes seemed so sad. He recognized this type of sadness, because he and his siblings had experienced it firsthand after his father left, leaving their mom to care for seven boys and a little girl all on her own.

And what about Abby? He'd had his chance all those years ago. She had moved on, got married, started a family. Maybe his father was right when he'd called Noah a pathetic loser. Noah banished the thought as he picked up the little puppy and held the tip of the bottle to his nose, letting it sniff a drop of milk. Then he dabbed a tiny bit on the dog's lip. The puppy didn't react at first, but then when Noah stuck his pinkie finger with a dab of the warm liquid inside the puppy's mouth, it started to drink.

"There you go, little one," Noah said under his breath, pulling his finger out of the dog's mouth and offering the bottle in its stead. A smile creased his lips as the little puppy started to pull at the bottle.

"Well done." He petted the pup's head as a warm feeling of hope filled his heart. The chances that this tiny dog would make it just increased dramatically. He ran his index finger down the puppy's back, warmth rising in his chest. For the first time all day, hope flickered. If this fragile creature could fight to live, maybe second chances weren't as impossible as they seemed. And maybe, just maybe, he could find a way to mend the broken places in his own life too.

Chapter Three

Once his shift at the vet clinic was over, Noah went home and collapsed on his sofa, still wearing his mint-green scrubs. What a night. The clinic hadn't been super busy, but taking care of the puppy, who needed constant attention, had tired him out. Once he fed the pup the cat milk supplement, it had rapidly recovered. Which meant that it was suddenly hungry. Noah had to feed it every twenty minutes. The puppy kept whining, looking for his mother and siblings and, of course, more food. Noah wondered how this little puppy had become an orphan, but there was no way to find out. Between the puppy, the scheduled appointment and a couple of late-night drop-ins, Noah had had no time to eat his takeout.

Just then, his stomach growled. Noah wondered if he should reheat his burger first, then take the dogs out, but knowing his Vizslas, they would sit right by his feet and watch him as he ate.

"Tell you what." He stood and reached for the leashes. Rosie and Briggs were instantly excited. "Let's go for a quick walk, and then we'll all have some food."

The dogs were at the door before he could finish his sentence. No one needed to explain to them what the leashes in Noah's hand meant. He clicked them into the rings on their collars.

"And if we see Brenda on the stairs, mind your own business. No sniffing her. Understood?"

Both dogs held his gaze, as if they comprehended his every word.

"Okay, let's go."

Plastic baggies stuffed in his pocket, Noah opened the door, and both of his companions darted out.

"Settle," he said in a calm tone, wrapping the leashes tight around his wrist. He made them both heel and then they all walked slowly down the stairs. Brenda was nowhere to be seen.

He was thankful for small mercies.

They all walked down the street together toward a small park. His dogs were full of unspent energy, ready for a proper run, but that would not be possible here. He made them walk next to him, allowing a little extra slack when they needed it.

Should he call Abby and see if she needed anything? Offer to come up to the cabin? Ask her if he could bring the dogs?

Noah sighed. Judging by the chilly reception he had received yesterday, that would probably be a little too much. He looked at his dogs. What should he do? He couldn't take them to a dog park, especially since Rosie was expecting puppies. And Briggs had been very protective of her lately. No telling how he would react to any other male dog coming near Rosie. Noah would have to figure out some other way to give his dogs a safe way to exercise.

Just then, his phone rang.

It was Abby.

"Good morning." He did his best to sound cheerful.

"Good morning. Hope I didn't wake you."

"No worries. What's up?"

"Noah, I'm at the loft above the coach house right now, and it seems that there's a lot of stuff here that belongs to you."

"Yeah, about that—"

"I thought we had a deal. You said, when I called you last month, that two weeks was plenty of time to move all of it out. So, could you swing by today and take some of these boxes with you?"

"Sure, what time works?"

"Any time is good. Charlotte and I'll be cleaning, so pop in whenever."

"Will do."

"Thanks."

The call disconnected so abruptly he had no chance to ask if he could bring the dogs with him. Charlotte would definitely have fun if he did. Noah smiled at the thought. And perhaps Abby would allow him to take them out for a run in the forest.

Noah patted Briggs, who sat patiently at his feet. Rosie was busy sniffing a tree.

"Okay, kids, time to head back, have some chow and, after a nap, we're heading up the mountain. Hope the weather holds." He could use much more than a short nap, but Abby needed him to move is stuff.

There was not a cloud in the sky, but that meant nothing in these mountains. The weather could change in the blink of an eye.

The trio walked back to the condo. Where would he put all that stuff? His apartment was already full. He would have to make some more calls and see if anyone in town had a garage for rent. Or he could talk to Abby and see if she would let him rent hers. After all, it was empty. But would she even consider it?

He'd have to wait and see.

Abby leaned back in one of the kitchen chairs. Had calling Noah and asking him to pick up his stuff been a good idea? If she were honest with herself, seeing him yesterday was nice. But she had more important things to think about than her high school boyfriend. She pushed the chair away from the table and got to her feet—time to check on Charlotte's progress.

"How is the unpacking going, sweetie?" Abby called down the hallway.

"We need to buy paint," her daughter replied. "The walls don't match any of my clothes."

Abby chuckled. Yes, her daughter had a very particular

taste—mainly all shades of pink. Perhaps she could ask Noah if Mr. Enzo's hardware store was still open.

She frowned. Why was she thinking of him again? The last time they'd had a meaningful conversation was the night of their high school prom—right before she caught him kissing her best friend, Natalie—who'd been his twin brother Brad's girlfriend. Her heart squeezed at the terrible memory. She had stepped out of the gym to go to the restroom for a moment, then realized that she'd left her phone in Noah's truck. That quick trip to the parking lot had changed her life.

There she'd seen Noah under the streetlight, Natalie in his arms. Abby thought she would faint right on the spot.

Her eyes misted at the memory of her first heartbreak. Would she ever be able to trust another man?

Abby leaned against the door frame to her childhood room and watched Charlotte carefully spread her pink garments over the old comforter. Nothing had changed since the summer of her high school graduation. Her parents had left it all as she had it, including the poster above her bed.

Her daughter took one of her pink T-shirts, stood on her tippy toes and spread it over the top of the pine dresser.

Abby waited to see where this was going.

Charlotte picked up another shirt and stretched it over the headboard. "Mom, can you get me some hair clips?"

"What are you doing?"

"Decorating, of course," Charlotte replied, as if shocked by Abby's question.

"With your T-shirts?"

"I'll have to make do until we paint. There is not enough pink in this room."

Abby tried her best to hold in a chuckle.

"Sweetie, just put your clothes away in the drawers, please."

Charlotte faced her, arms crossed over her chest.

"You said this is my room. And if this is my room, I want to decorate it my way."

Was this worth a fight? How much did it really matter that Charlotte's clothes would be all over her room until they were able to purchase a couple of gallons of pink paint?

"Okay," Abby glanced at the floor. "And what about this one?" She pointed to a soft pink hoodie crumpled by Charlotte's bed.

"I'm wearing that."

"In the house?"

Charlotte blew out her cheeks. "No, Mom. Out-side." She split the word into two syllables.

"Well, in that case, why don't you pick it up and hang it on the hooks in the hallway."

"I will, but first I have to finish decorating."

Abby gave in with a sigh, deciding to leave her daughter's interior design alone and make herself another cup of coffee. Her eyes scanned the room once more. Repainting it would be something she needed to prepare for. The memories seemed to be everywhere—including the wall paint. Mom and Dad had let her choose it. It had been fall, and she'd wanted the color to match the autumn leaves—so light brown it was. She felt so mature choosing it, instead of the girly pink or purple.

Abby would have to tell Charlotte about the construction of this house. Her father had sold his law firm, and Mom, a magazine ad designer, had decided to work from home, before it was something everyone could do. They'd bought this land when Abby was about the same age as Charlotte. A smile touched the corners of her lips, then the stab of pain instantly took all the joy away.

"I'll be in the living room, if you need anything. Mr. Ross will stop by later."

"Who is Mr. Ross?" Charlotte shot her a look, a pink jacket in her hands.

"The man that you met yesterday."

"He said his name was Noah."

"Yes, his name is Noah Ross."

"How do you know him?" Charlotte asked as she spread the jacket over the forest-print pillow.

"Since we were kids. But you can't sleep on that." She pointed at the jacket.

"Only until we get pink sheets, Mom. This cover gave me bad dreams."

"All right," Abby sighed, deciding it was definitely time for that coffee.

Life would have been so much easier if her parents were still alive. They could have all fit into this house. Or Abby and Charlotte could move into the loft apartment above the detached garage. It would have been wonderful to live right next door to her parents. But she wouldn't think of that now.

Abby reached into the cupboard. The matching mugs Noah had bought for them the last Valentine's Day they had spent together were still there. Why had he not thrown them out, or taken them with all his stuff? She'd given him plenty of notice.

Abby filled the kettle and turned it on. She leaned against the counter and waited for the water to boil. Her eyes traveled over the surfaces, walls and countless little knickknacks—why had he kept all this stuff around for this long? It had been ten years since a drunk driver had killed her parents. Right after their funeral, Noah had asked Abby if she would let him move from the loft apartment above the detached garage into the cabin, since she didn't want to rent it to anyone else. She assumed he would have gotten rid of all of her parents' things, either donated them, or packed them away for her to sort through one day. But it was all here, seemingly just as Mom and Dad had left it. Why?

Abby picked up the jar of instant decaf. What had Noah been up to since the summer after high school graduation, when she had moved to St. Louis, excited to start college—and even more eager to put the prom night disaster behind her? She hadn't even said goodbye to her friends, so desperate was she to leave Hope Rock, Colorado, behind and start a new life.

Abby poured the hot water over the dark crystals. The black liquid rose to the rim. She should have visited when her parents asked her to come home for the holidays. But Abby had blamed the distance and schoolwork, not wanting them to find out about her new boyfriend, Ken. What a whirlwind romance that had been. A deep sigh escaped her. A dab of milk from the fridge, a quick stir—Abby carried her mug into the living room. Sinking into the sofa cushions, she took a sip.

Ken. The second-biggest mistake of her life. Charming and sweet—he'd love-bombed her right from the start. Her broken heart was so eager to find love that she had ignored all the red flags.

She was barely eighteen, and he was six years her senior. Abby had felt so mature dating him. Ken had been enrolled in a postgrad program at her school. A financial genius, he'd had tons of job offers lined up even before his graduation. During her sophomore year, Ken had told her he'd make enough money for the two of them, and there was no reason for her to struggle through of the rest of college if all she wanted was to be married and have children.

She'd agreed with him wholeheartedly.

When she broke the news to her parents that she was dropping out of college and getting married, they'd urged her to come home. She mailed them a wedding invitation instead. Dad had walked her down the aisle, squeezing her hand.

Wrapped up in her new life, Abby seemed too busy to visit them. She still called on a regular basis, but had to turn down even their Christmas invitations, as Ken wasn't keen on Colorado winters. When she phoned them right after she and Ken had returned from celebrating their third anniversary in the

Bahamas and told them their first grandchild was on the way, they were overjoyed.

But when the next call from Colorado came, it wasn't from her parents. It was Noah. He had been living in the loft apartment above the detached garage, helping her dad to take care of the property. She hadn't spoken to him since the prom night, so she was a little surprised that he'd called. When he started to explain the news, Abby's heart instantly filled with fear. Her parents had been in a car accident. They were gone. Back then, she'd had Ken to lean on, and he'd taken care of most of the arrangements. But when he'd insisted that Abby sell the cabin, something told her not to. That had been the first time she had disagreed with her husband, and things had unraveled ever since.

Abby sipped her drink. Ken was gone. How was she going to get through this? She and Charlotte had arrived only yesterday, and already all the old memories were overwhelming her.

All she could do was take things one step at a time, right?

Chapter Four

Tuesday morning, washing up after breakfast, Abby looked out the kitchen window just in time to see Noah's red pickup pull up to the house. Her chest felt a little tight as Noah jumped out of the cab, his Stetson shielding his eyes. He reached for the back door and let out his dogs.

"Mommy." Charlotte sprinted into the kitchen. "Mr. Noah is here, and he brought the big doggies."

"I see that." Abby's gaze wandered back outside. "I want you to be careful around the dogs. They seem a bit wild."

"I'm not scared of them." Charlotte lifted her chin. "They love me."

"They do?"

"Yep. And I know it. Right here." She pressed her hand right over her heart.

"But ask Mr. Noah—"

"Ask what?" Charlotte stopped at the door and grabbed the soft pink hoodie she'd obediently hung up from the hook by the front door.

"For permission, of course."

"I will. Thanks, Mom."

Watching the blond ponytail sway as Charlotte ran out the door into the sunshine made Abby smile. Maybe this was good for her daughter. But Abby needed to clear up a few things with

Noah first. She wiped her hands with a dishcloth, leaned onto the counter and breathed a short prayer.

Lord, please give me wisdom.

Then Abby walked to the front door and opened it.

"Hi."

There he stood, right in front of her.

"I was just about to knock."

"Saved you the effort," she said as she stepped forward, claiming her personal space. The door shut behind her with a resolute thud. Abby looked around the front yard. "Where's Charlotte?"

"Over there." Noah strode toward the detached garages. "Look." He motioned toward the side yard.

Charlotte stood there, a yellow Frisbee in her hand, two eager Vizslas watching her every move.

"I said you have to sit first, Briggs." She sounded a lot like her first-grade teacher. "I'll throw the Frisbee, but only if you listen."

Briggs sat next to Rosie.

"Much better." She patted the dog on his head.

His tongue scored a quick lick.

"Thank you for the kiss." She smiled. "Ready?" With a flick of her right wrist, the Frisbee sailed through the air. The dogs took off running. Briggs got it first, then ran a few circles around Rosie, who tried to snatch it out of his mouth. Charlotte laughed.

It filled Abby with joy to hear the sweet sound of her daughter laughing.

"Thank you, Noah," she said softly.

"For what?"

"I haven't seen her this happy in months." Looking at him, her breath caught.

No. Absolutely not.

She wouldn't go there. Ever.

"Coming to get your stuff?" She struggled to sound casual,

as if she had forgotten it was she who had called him to come up and pick up his stuff only a few short hours ago.

He held her gaze for a few seconds before he spoke.

"I would like to run a couple of things by you."

"Mommy! Look!" Charlotte called out. "Watch this. Briggs. Give."

The dog trotted toward her, placed the Frisbee at Charlotte's feet, sat on his haunches and waited. Rosie followed his lead. Charlotte picked up the Frisbee. "Ready?"

The disk flew through the air, and the dogs chased after it.

"You got the hang of it," Noah said. "Great job, Charlotte."

"Listen, I've got to get going. There's a lot I need to get done," Abby made an excuse. "What did you need?"

"I would like to ask you a couple of favors."

She frowned.

"Would it be at all possible to leave some of my stuff in the garage? It would only be for a few days." Noah lifted his hands in mock surrender. "I'm having a hard time finding a storage place."

Abby was silent for a moment. If she said yes, would he be up here every other day?

She glanced at her daughter. On the other hand, maybe playing with his dogs was exactly what Charlotte needed. Abby could cope with seeing Noah often if it meant he brought the dogs for her daughter to play with.

"Okay, but only a week or so. I need to clean up the loft so Charlotte and I can stay there while we renovate the cabin."

"I can help you move stuff around, if you'd like."

"Thanks, but we'll be fine."

The last thing Abby wanted was Noah nearby as she sorted through her old high school yearbooks, filled with memories of the two of them.

"What's the second favor you need?"

His eyes followed the Frisbee. "I wanted to ask if you would be okay with me bringing the dogs up here to exercise them. My condo is so small, and they aren't used to being on the leash."

Abby sighed. She had promised herself the day she signed the divorce papers that she would do things differently, be firm and clear about what she wanted. Would allowing Noah to come up to the cabin any time it suited him be a wise decision? But as she searched his eyes for a hint of malice, she found none.

"Hey, if it's a problem, just say so. I don't want to bother you." Noah adjusted his Stetson.

"It's no bother," she said. "But what worries me is Charlotte."

"Charlotte?" Noah glanced in the little girl's direction. "She looks happy to me. The dogs love her."

"Precisely."

Noah stood still, as if frozen to the ground. What did she mean by that? Was she still holding some old grudge all these years later? It had been her decision not to talk things out before she left town for college. No one knew why she had stopped talking to all her friends. How many times had he driven up this mountain trying to figure out what had happened, without success? Or did she think that he was trying to win over her daughter to get closer to her?

"Abby," he said, "if you think that I'm creating a problem here, letting Charlotte play with the dogs, just come out and say it. No need to play games."

"Charlotte," she called out to her daughter. "Noah is leaving now. Say goodbye to the dogs."

"Abby," he said under his breath. "If you don't want me around, I won't bother you."

She looked at him straight on. "I have a daughter to think of. Yes, she likes your dogs, and she likes you, too, but her heart has been broken recently by someone she trusted and loved. I promised myself that I wouldn't allow another man to do that to her again, as long as I live."

"I understand. But that's not my intent. If she enjoys a few minutes with the dogs, I see no harm in that."

"Don't tell me how to raise my daughter."

"Abby—"

"Charlotte. Come on!"

"One more throw, Mom. Please?"

Abby let out a deep sigh. "Okay, just one more, but then we've got to let Noah go. He must have things to do."

"Listen to me," Noah said quietly. "I'm here to help. Just be honest with me and tell me what works and what doesn't. If you're going to be upset every time I stop by, then naturally, bringing my dogs here for a run won't work."

She glanced at him.

"For either of us," he added.

She remained silent, her face hard.

"I don't mean to hurt your feelings, Abby. You've obviously been through a tough time, and I want to help you. That's if you want me to. If not, say the word. No hard feelings."

Abby wrapped her arms around her midsection.

"I… I don't know." When she looked up, her eyes glistened. "I'm sorry to come across so harsh. But the divorce was really hard on her."

"And you?" he said in a low voice.

She nodded.

"Okay. I get it. Let's play by your rules."

She glanced over at her daughter, and a tiny smile crossed her lips.

"Thank you."

"All right." He touched his hat, then called out, "Briggs, Rosie, heel."

The dogs ran over to him and sat at his left foot.

"Good job." He petted them and offered each a small treat. "Stay."

Noah walked over to Charlotte and retrieved the Frisbee.

"Thank you for playing with them."

"Can you come again tomorrow?" Her eyes sparkled with anticipation.

"I'll have to ask your mom if tomorrow works for her. You guys might be busy."

"We're not busy at all." Charlotte tilted her head. "All we did yesterday was drive and unpack. And cleaning all day today is no fun."

He chuckled. "Let me talk to her and see what would work."

"Mommy!" Charlotte ran toward Abby. "Can Noah bring the dogs tomorrow?"

Noah chuckled. He had no intention of making the situation between him and Abby any worse. Truth be told, he really needed her to say yes to his requests, as the storage situation in Hope Rock was pretty dire. Then there was the condo-rules problem.

He sauntered over to Abby, Frisbee in hand.

"Okay, we'll be on our way," he said.

"So, are you coming tomorrow, Mr. Noah?" Charlotte asked with excitement in her voice.

Noah looked at Abby, waiting for her response.

"Say yes, Mr. Noah. Pleeease." Charlotte was jumping up and down. The dogs, excited by this, ran in circles around the three of them.

"That's up to your mom, sweetie."

When Abby remained silent, he got the picture loud and clear. He called the dogs over to him and opened his truck door.

"Briggs, Rosie." The dogs obeyed and jumped onto the back seats. Noah shut the door behind them. He touched the rim of his hat, then curtly nodded.

The smile on Charlotte's face was part wonder and part delight.

"They are so smart," she said under her breath.

Abby reached for her hand.

"As I've said before, call me if you need anything." Noah opened his truck. "You have my number."

"Wait, Noah," Abby called out, her voice a little shaky. "What time would work for you tomorrow?"

He whispered a quick prayer of thanks.

"I work the night shift for the rest of the week. Then I need to pick up these guys." He motioned toward the Vizslas. "I could be here around ten thirty in the morning, if that's okay?"

"Sure," Abby said.

"Yay!" Charlotte clapped her hands. "Mommy, can we bake dog cookies for tomorrow?"

"Dog cookies?"

"Yeah, just like I watched on YouTube. We can look up the recipe."

"No need to go to any trouble," Noah interrupted. "They'll be just as happy if you let them run around."

"Okay. Ten thirty, then," Abby said.

"Great." He hoisted himself into the truck. "Thanks. See you tomorrow." He started his engine, but before he turned around, he rolled down his window. "Need anything in town?"

"No, thanks. We're good."

"A latte?" His lips curled up in a mischievous grin.

"You know that I can't say no to that." Abby chuckled.

"A latte it is," he said and gave her his signature wave.

As he drove down the mountain, he gave thanks that Abby was finally opening up a little.

Chapter Five

Abby walked with Charlotte back into the house, and when her daughter rushed to the bathroom to wash her hands, Abby leaned against the front door.

What had she agreed to? Maybe she should call Noah right now and cancel their arrangement, tell him it wouldn't work. But he'd see through that in an instant. He'd asked her to be honest with him. But honesty required trust. And the only person Abby trusted was herself—and Charlotte, of course.

She pushed off the door. Okay, time for a cup of coffee. She smiled. Noah had remembered her affinity for a good latte. Was there a way to rebuild some of the trust that had been lost between them all those years ago? Would she even be able to do that while healing from a shattered heart?

"Mommy." Charlotte ran into the room. "Can we make the dog cookies?"

"But we have to finish unpacking today."

Charlotte made a face. "That's so boring."

"It has to be done."

Her sweet daughter flopped on the sofa. "Why?"

"So, we can settle in."

"Can we settle in after we bake the doggie cookies? Pleeease? I copied the recipe."

One long sigh later, Abby stretched out her arm. "Let me see."

Charlotte handed her a piece of paper covered with lines of carefully printed letters in bright Crayon colors.

"Can we, Mommy?" Charlotte asked, jumping with excitement. The girl had so much energy today.

"Well, we do have flour and peanut butter. The eggs are in the fridge. I'm not sure about the baking powder."

"Can we skip that?"

"I don't know, sweetie. They may not turn out well if we do."

"Can you call Mr. Noah to bring us some?"

"Charlotte, we can't just call him every time we need something."

"Can we go pick it up, so we don't bother him?"

"I don't think so. We'll drive to Hope Rock and get some shopping done on Saturday. Remember, we're still working on our list."

"Saturdaaayyy?" Charlotte stretched out the word. "But I want to bake the dog cookies today," she whined.

"What did I tell you about using that tone?"

Abby couldn't keep giving in to everything Charlotte wanted. It only made things worse in the long run.

"Listen, why don't you finish unpacking the rest of your things? I'll make us some nice hot chocolate, and then we can sit down with a calendar and plan out the rest of this week."

"But I want to bake doggie cookies!"

Abby struggled to keep her emotions in check, unwilling to raise her voice to her daughter.

"Charlotte," she enunciated with exaggeration, "please go unpack your stuff now. I'll make hot chocolate for us, and while the water is heating up, I could check the pantry and see if there is any baking powder tucked away in some corner or drawer we missed. But only if you do what I've asked."

"Okay, Mommy," Charlotte capitulated and ran back upstairs.

Abby opened the fridge, and as she reached for the carton

of milk, her thoughts wandered. The man who'd so thoughtfully stocked up her refrigerator was very different from the boy she remembered. Naturally, he looked more mature, and his frame had filled out.

Abby shook her head. Absolutely no way would she allow herself to think of Noah in any other way than as a former tenant. And as the owner of two rambunctious dogs her daughter happened to like—a lot.

She poured the milk into the saucepan, turned on the stove and adjusted the flame.

"Mom, is the hot chocolate ready yet?" Charlotte's voice carried from her room and pulled her out of her thoughts. How would she ever be able to express her gratitude for this wonderful child?

"Two more minutes, sweetheart."

"I'm done first. I beat you!" Charlotte sprinted into the kitchen. "Can I get the ingredients from the pantry?"

"Sure," she replied and reached into the cupboard for a mug. Her hand froze midair—the Valentine's Day mugs. Perhaps they should start a donation box and declutter the house. Her eyes lingered on hers.

Love never fails.

The scrawled-font letters were clearly legible. Her mug looked almost new. She reached for his. They had once matched, but now the writing had faded, as if it had been used a million times. She opened the cupboard door under the sink and lifted the trash can lid. There were plenty of other items to donate. There was no time like the present to cleanse the house of all unpleasant memories.

"Mom," Charlotte rushed toward her. "Where can I put the flour?" She glanced at the mug. "Why are you throwing that out?"

"I don't like it."

"But it's so pretty. Can I have it?"

Abby blew out her cheeks. This was the last thing she had imagined. How was she to say no? "It's kind of old. Why don't I buy you a new one on Saturday?"

"But it's pink. I love pink. And I love hearts. This is the most nicest mug in the cupboard." Her eyes traveled to the open door. "Oh, and there's a matching one. That one looks new. Can I have that one, and you keep this one, and we'll have matching hot chocolate mugs?"

"Okay." Abby gave it to her daughter.

"Yay! I found my apron. I'll put it on, and as soon as we're finished with the hot chocolate, we can start baking. Okay?"

"Of course, honey." Abby smiled but felt no warmth. She would bake dog cookies with her daughter in a kitchen full of memories of her parents—while sipping hot chocolate from her ex-boyfriend's mug.

Noah attached the leashes to the dogs' collars and led them to the back door of the condo building.

He thought of Abby. How much pain was stored up in her heart? Would she let God step in? Because of the way things were right now, Noah was definitely not her choice of prayer partner. But that wouldn't stop him from praying for her. And Charlotte. That sweet girl was full of life, and from what he had observed, her little heart was starting to mend. She genuinely loved the dogs, and the pure joy of their interactions was so sweet.

As he reached the door, he noticed a yellow sticky note. He crumpled it into his pocket without reading it.

The dogs rushed into the apartment. Toeing off his shoes, he walked into the living room. Noah picked up his coffee mug from the edge of the side table and headed toward the kitchen, the dogs following him.

"Breakfast time." He patted Rosie's head, then picked up their bowls off the floor. He filled the electric kettle and flicked the switch. While he scooped the coffee granules for himself and sprinkled dry liver dust over their food for an extra treat, the water boiled.

Noah poured hot water over the coffee in a clean mug and stirred it with yesterday's spoon. Standing by the window, he looked down at the street below. He couldn't see the mountains from here. His thoughts returned to Abby. And Charlotte. A part of him wanted to charge in and fix everything that was broken. But healing took time. It didn't come from forced answers to life's problems. It came from showing up again and again with steady kindness. With prayer. And with patience. He covered a yawn with the back of his hand. The night shift loomed, and he needed to rest. Still, as he set the mug aside and headed for the couch, one truth stayed with him—if he kept showing up, maybe one day they would let him close enough to try again. Maybe love wasn't about grand gestures after all, but about the quiet persistence of being there when it mattered most.

Chapter Six

Wednesday morning was dark, and so was Abby's mood. She looked out the window observing the heavy clouds hiding the mountain peaks. So much had happened in the two short days since she parked her car in front of her cabin. As she tried to sort through the jumble of her emotions, she couldn't help but wonder how had she thought that allowing Noah to come up here any time he wanted would be a good idea? And what about the dogs? They were a handful, but they brought so much joy to her daughter. Abby had no idea how to stop Noah's visits without hurting the person who was most precious to her in the entire world. Charlotte was quickly falling in love with the two dogs, and judging by the size of Rosie's belly, there would soon be more animals to love.

There was no way the dogs could stay here once the puppies were born. But perhaps cute and cuddly puppies, full of energy, were what Charlotte needed the most right now.

She glanced at the pillow next to her. Her sweet girl slept curled up, holding onto a stuffed animal. Abby would do anything for her daughter. If that meant having a pack of dogs running through the house, she would put up with that, too, if only to hear that giggly laughter again.

Sitting up, Abby tried to make as little noise as possible as she walked toward the bathroom. Perhaps she could get ready before her daughter woke up, maybe even make herself a cup of coffee and sit on the back porch. It was sheltered from the rain. And if she grabbed a blanket from the living room, she could cozy up and prepare for the day—maybe even pray.

Abby pulled the faucet handle upward. Nothing. She frowned. Then tried again.

No water.

She went to the kitchen and tested the faucet there. Not a drop.

She looked around the kitchen. They still had the open pack of water bottles from their car trip. That would have to do for now. Abby picked one up, walked back to the bathroom and brushed her teeth.

Back in the kitchen, she poured the contents of another bottle into the kettle and turned on the stove. At least the propane was working. While the water heated, Abby went back to the bedroom and took her phone from the charging station.

At least the power had stayed on all night.

With Noah's old Valentine's Day mug in hand, Abby reached for a blanket. Her purple cotton pajamas were definitely not warm enough to wear on a cool summer morning high up in the mountains.

She carefully opened the door to the back porch. It squeaked. She paused and listened. No sound. Charlotte was still asleep. Abby sneaked outside. The rough, weathered chair sat on the porch, inviting her to sit down and take in the beauty of this place. Its frame was shaped by hand rather than machine, and the wood bore the marks of time—splintered edges, knots that told stories, and grain raised by years of mountain wind and sun. Her dad used to sit in it and read his Bible. Abby settled in, and wrapped the blanket around herself. She held the mug with both hands and inhaled the aroma. Coffee had the power to bring her instant comfort. Most people used the brew to give them a jolt of energy, but not her. She sought this drink for a sense of balance in life. But what kind of balance could an old mug offer to her now, when they were without water, up in the mountains, and the only person who could help her was her ex-boyfriend, whom she really didn't want to talk to this early in the morning?

Her life was such a mess. She took her first sip. If only a cup of coffee could solve all her problems. She looked out at the view. How could she have forgotten how beautiful this place was?

She took another sip. Gentle drops of rain drummed on the roof sheltering the deck. It was all so peaceful. Was this why her parents had picked this place to build their dream house?

They'd been so happy here. They'd built their family, gotten involved in the church, kept busy with their jobs, but most of all, they'd loved God.

She frowned.

Sometimes I don't understand faith at all. I look at my parents, and they lived for You, God. And yet, You let them die in a terrible crash. Is this how You reward those who follow You?

She gritted her teeth. Maybe that wasn't fair. Could she blame God for someone's decision to drink and drive?

Inhaling the scent of her coffee, she took another sip. She felt so lonely, lost and overwhelmed. And now, she had no water in the house. She needed to find a solution—and fast.

She glanced at her phone. Noah would know what to do.

Abby's number flashed on the screen of his phone. He put down his coffee and reached for it.

"Good morning. Is everything okay?"

"Hey, Noah. Sorry to call you this early. But I've got a problem. The water isn't running in the house. Is there something I can do to turn it back on?"

"Have you checked the well pump?"

"The well pump?"

"Okay, I've got a couple of things to finish up before the day shift comes in, but I can swing by right after and check on it."

"You're at work?"

"Yes, I do have a job," he chuckled.

"Where do you work?"

"At the Hope Rock Veterinary Clinic."

The phone went silent. Had the call been disconnected? It happened from time to time; it was a hazard of living in the mountains.

"Abby? Are you there?"

"Sorry. I guess I'm a bit surprised. I don't remember you ever talking about wanting to be a vet tech."

Noah decided not to correct her. "Well, we haven't really spoken since high school. A lot has changed since then," Noah responded.

"I'm happy for you," she said, breaking the silence.

There was so much sadness in it, Noah's heart ached.

"Abby, are you okay?"

"Yes. It's just that I feel as if everyone around me had a life and I was in limbo for all these years."

"What do you mean? You got your degree, got married and built a family." Maybe this wasn't the best choice of words. "Sorry, I don't mean to sound insensitive. I know the divorce is hard on you and Charlotte, but look at her. That kid is pretty amazing."

"She certainly is," she said.

"Okay, let me finish up here. I should be there in about an hour."

"Noah?"

"Yes?"

"Sorry for being so…standoffish. I've got a lot on my mind and—"

"No need to apologize."

"Thanks. Will you bring the dogs with you?"

Noah hesitated. Was this an invitation or a polite way to ask him to leave them at home?

"Should I?"

"Please do. Charlotte will be so happy to see them."

"Great, we'll see you soon."

Noah disconnected the call and took a deep breath. The water pump probably kicked the breaker, so that should be a quick fix, but what surprised him was Abby's invitation to bring Rosie and Briggs.

He opened a folder and finished the paperwork he was working on. It had been a busy night at the clinic. Noah glanced at the kennel in the corner of the examination room. The puppy seemed quite content in the new box, lined with towels and comfortable under the heat lamp. The staff was more than willing to keep up with the feeding schedule, and the little dog seemed to grow by the hour.

The county dog rescue center had finally gotten back to him. Unfortunately, they weren't able to take the puppy now. It was too young for their facility. They had promised to look for an alternative placement in another shelter, but that would take a while. That left Noah with only one option. He didn't want to call his twin brother, Brad, and ask him for yet another favor. But if Cindy didn't find a place for the stray pup, hopefully Brad would have a spot in the no-kill shelter he managed in River Run. The puppy would be fine here for a day or two more, but it was only a question of time before his boss would ask for it to be transferred to a more suitable facility.

Noah stacked the files, picked up the bundle and walked to the reception area. The day staff would handle all the billing and file everything away.

Just then, the front door opened. Noah looked up, expecting another emergency. To his great relief, Cindy walked in, her coffee in hand.

"I'm glad to see you. Thanks for coming in early. Something just came up, and I need to take off as soon as possible."

"The puppies?" Cindy set down her coffee.

"No, Rosie still has a few days to go, but a friend just called asking for help."   .

"For sure, I can hold down the fort. Dr. Gina should be here—" Cindy glanced at her watch "—in less than twenty minutes."

"Thank you. But if anything comes up, call me and I'll swing right back."

"No worries. And pet the little momma for me."

"Will do."

Noah patted his pockets, checking for the truck keys.

"I fed the puppy and made notes on the chart. Thank you for setting that up. It's good to keep track of his progress." Noah hesitated.

Cindy looked up. "Is there anything else?"

"No, I—"

"Dr. Ross, just get out of here. I got this."

He chuckled. "I know, I know. Thank you, Cindy."

Noah stepped out into the fresh mountain morning—there were a few wispy clouds gathered around the peaks. The day looked promising. Cool wind blew through his green scrubs. He would need to change and grab a jacket before going to Abby's place. Noah exited the parking lot and drove in the direction of his condo. Could he talk to Abby about the puppies today? He hated to impose on her, but everything had happened so fast that it left him with only a few options. Had he known that Abby needed the house, he would not have planned for pups. Puppies were such a wonderful blessing, but so much work, and his condo was definitely no place to raise a litter of Vizslas. But he didn't want her to think that he was taking advantage of her. How best to handle this?

He'd leave it in God's hands…

Chapter Seven

She didn't like that she had to call Noah for help. He had offered several times, but Abby didn't want to be dependent on
anyone—not even Noah. But who else could she ask? They
needed running water, and Noah had lived here for the past ten
years. He knew this house better than anyone else.

"Mom!" A panicked scream jolted Abby to her feet. The coffee sloshed all over the blanket.

"Charlotte?" Her hand flew up and pushed against the porch
door. Abby looked around the kitchen. "Charlotte!"

The sleepy girl walked toward her barefoot, a stuffed animal under her arm.

"Where were you? I thought you had left me."

"I'm here, sweetie. I'm here." Abby knelt in front of her child
and wrapped her arms around her.

"I woke up and you were gone. I got scared."

"Shh," Abby soothed her sobbing daughter. "I was just out
on the deck—" she pointed in that direction "—having coffee."

"I thought you were gone."

"Sweetheart—" She hugged her even closer. "I would never
leave you. You're my everything." Abby took her daughter's
face in her hands. "I'm here, and there is no need to be afraid.
And you know what?"

"What?"

"I've got a little surprise for you."

"A surprise? What surprise?"

"What would you say if I told you Mr. Noah was on his way over, and he's bringing Briggs and Rosie with him?"

Charlotte's tear-streaked face lit up.

"I'll go get changed and brush my teeth."

"About that. The water isn't running. But Noah knows how to fix it."

"He does?" The girl's eyes grew wide. "Mr. Noah's pretty smart, isn't he, Mom?"

Abby stifled a sigh. "Yep. Go get changed and let's figure out breakfast before he gets here."

Charlotte ran back into the bedroom, but before Abby could walk to the fridge to see what she could make for them to eat that wouldn't require much water, Charlotte was back. And she hadn't changed clothes yet.

"Can Mr. Noah have breakfast with us?"

How could she tell her daughter that there was no room for him at their table? Wouldn't that be against every value she tried to model for her? But as kind and helpful as Noah had been, he was still the first man who broke her heart.

"I don't know. He may have eaten breakfast already."

Charlotte's brow furrowed.

"And I'm not sure how long he can stay, since he just got off work. He may be really tired."

"But what if he's really hungry, too?"

There were times when Abby admired Charlotte's persistence—and then there were situations like this.

"I know." Charlotte's enthusiasm bubbled over. "I'll set the table for three, and if he's already eaten, he could just sit and watch us."

"Watch us?"

"Yes. Watch us eat. And wait till I'm done, so Rosie and Briggs can play with me right after breakfast."

Abby shook her head slightly.

"Having someone watch you eat isn't very polite. Why don't we eat now before he gets here?"

"But what if he's hungry?"

There was no winning this argument.

"All right." Abby pulled at the refrigerator door. "I'll see what I can scrounge up."

"Pancakes!"

"Pancakes?"

"Yes. You make the best pancakes ever, and Noah will surely like them, even if he isn't hungry."

It was impossible to argue with that. Abby opened the cupboard door and took out the pancake mix. She set the eggs, milk and butter on the counter.

"All right, *now* go get changed."

Charlotte sprinted toward her bedroom, and before Abby could measure out the ingredients, she was back.

The pink ensemble she'd chosen and the cute, messy ponytail her daughter had managed to clip in a pink bow were downright adorable.

"Can I help you, Mommy?"

"Of course."

"I'll crack the eggs."

Abby stopped herself before she let out the discouraging words that sat on the tip of her tongue.

"Here, crack them into this bowl," Abby said, taking one from the cupboard. "That way, you don't need to worry if a piece of shell falls in. We can take it out with a spoon before adding the eggs to the pancake mix."

"Okay," Charlotte replied. "I'll be careful."

"I know you will." Abby ran her fingers down the swinging ponytail. "I like the bow in your hair."

"Thank you. Now watch me." Charlotte took an egg from the carton and carefully tapped it on the edge of the bowl. "Why is it not cracking?"

"You need to do it a little harder."

Charlotte nodded and then smashed the egg on the edge of the dish. It broke into three pieces, and the runny part spilled onto the counter.

Abby gasped and glanced around the kitchen, searching for a paper towel.

"I'm sorry, Mommy," Charlotte said, looking up, her voice quivering. The egg white dripped onto the floor.

"It's just an egg, sweetheart," Abby said in a soothing tone. "Let me wipe it." With a wad of paper towels in hand, Abby got to her knees and wiped up the mess.

Charlotte took the little dish and set it against the edge of the countertop. She used her index finger to push the yolk into the bowl, but it slipped, following the track the egg whites created. It landed on Abby's head and broke.

Abby froze as the ruined egg dripped down her hair and onto her hands. Great. And she had no way to get that out before Noah showed up. By the time he'd fixed the water, it would harden, making it impossible to rinse out. Hopefully, her pajamas weren't completely ruined.

Her stomach twisted, and she had to bite her tongue to stop the torrent of angry words. Charlotte stood there, obviously unsure of what to do next.

"It's okay." Abby got up and reached for a fresh paper towel, then wiped at the ends of her hair. She would need to change anyway before Noah knocked at the door. Maybe this wasn't such a huge disaster. The egg stain would surely come out.

"I'm sorry." Charlotte started to cry.

"Honey, it's only an egg." Abby forced a smile on her face. "Here, let me show you," she said, tossing the sticky paper towel into the garbage can under the sink. Abby took another egg out of the carton. "Why don't I crack it and then you try to open it into the bowl?"

"Okay."

The insecurity Abby noticed in her daughter's voice stung. Her child's fragile state evidently couldn't handle her disapproval.

"See—" Abby tapped the shell against the edge "—it only takes a bit of practice to learn how hard to hit the egg."

A crack.

"Here, you take over and open the shell." Abby handed the egg to Charlotte. Her little fingers were still messy from the failed attempt.

"Now use your thumbs. Stick them into the opening and pull the shell apart."

"Like this?" Charlotte split the shell. The yolk and the whites successfully landed inside the bowl. "I did it!"

Abby hugged her, despite the egg on her clothes. Who cared about laundry? The little victory was more important.

"Great job!"

Charlotte wrapped her arms around Abby.

"Can I do another one?"

"Why don't we do the next one together, so you can feel how much strength is needed to crack the shell just right?"

Working together, Charlotte finally got the hang of it.

"Great job, sweetheart. We have all the eggs we need. Now, let's measure the milk, then whisk it all together. Do you think you can help me with that? I'll get changed in the meantime."

"I can do that."

Her girl's enthusiasm returned. She carefully poured the milk into the measuring cup, then found a whisk in one of the drawers and slowly mixed the ingredients.

"Mr. Noah will love these," she said with a smile when Abby returned.

"I'm sure he will," Abby said and smiled. Her fuchsia toenails peeked out from the fraying hems of her old jeans, matching her bright T-shirt, sporting a big fluffy kitten. Charlotte had picked it out for her birthday. "I'll heat the frying pan," she added and tied her hair up in a messy bun. She cut a piece of butter and let it melt slowly.

"Is this okay, Mom?"

The batter was full of lumps and bits. "Almost. Give it a few more stirs."

"Big ones?"

"Try medium." Abby chuckled.

Charlotte gripped the whisk handle and used her whole arm to mix the thickening batter.

"It's getting harder."

"You're doing fine."

A knock on the door interrupted their conversation.

"It's Mr. Noah!" Charlotte let go of the whisk. "I'll get the door."

Before Abby could say a word, Charlotte ran to the front door and pulled it open.

"Good morning," Noah said, his voice filling the house.

"Hi. Where is Rosie?"

"In the truck."

"And Briggs?"

"Sitting right next to her." Noah chuckled.

"We're making pancakes for you."

"You are?"

"We're making breakfast," Abby said, walking toward the front door. Damage control was necessary so that Noah wouldn't get the wrong idea. "You can join us if you like. Come on in."

He stepped inside and closed the door, his presence suddenly filling the room.

"As promised." He handed her a latte. There was a Roasted Bean logo stamped on the side of the cup.

"Thank you, you have no idea how much I need this." She gave him an appreciative smile and immediately took a sip.

"Hope it didn't get cold. I asked for extra hot."

"It's perfect." Abby grinned. She was glad to see that Hope Rock had a place to get good coffee.

"It's a great spot. I'm sure you would like it." His gaze caught hers, and she had to avert her eyes before he noticed the heat rising to her cheeks.

Abby dropped her gaze. His western boots—they were the exact pair she had bought for him some twelve years ago. She smiled, and sneaked one more glance at those wide shoulders of his and hoped he didn't notice.

"Are they going to be okay?" Charlotte asked.

"Who?" Abby looked at Noah.

"She means the dogs. Yes, they are. It's not hot, and as soon as I check on the water pump, we can take them out." He glanced up at Abby. "That is, if your mom says it's okay."

"Can we, Mom?"

Abby forced a smile. "Of course." She had not planned on Noah staying longer than necessary, but seeing Charlotte so excited about the two dogs made her smile. Her daughter could use a bit of carefree fun—and Noah and his dogs seemed more than happy to offer it.

Noah had entered this house a thousand times, yet today, it felt like the first time. Abby stood in the hallway, her arms crossed. She seemed visibly uncomfortable. But her icy demeanor melted away as soon as he handed her the ladder. Her smile warmed his heart. Charlotte was glad to see him. Her eyes sparkled with excitement. He was sure that if Abby let her, she would sprint right to the truck and let the dogs out.

"Thank you for coming to check on the water pump," Abby said, walking back to the kitchen.

"No problem."

He would do what was needed and then go. The truth was that the lack of sleep was starting to get to him. Everything that had happened over the past few days was beginning to add up, and exhaustion was slowly setting in. Yet, he would do the best he could to help her out. Or so he'd promised himself on the way up this mountain. "All right." His eyes searched Abby's. "Let me check the pump and I'll be out of here."

"But—" Charlotte started to tear up. "We made you pancakes."

"And that's very nice of you." Noah tousled her hair, hoping that Abby would not take offense at that. "But I'm really tired. I've been working all night."

"You work at night?" Her eyes were filled with tears, but he could tell she was trying to be brave. "Where?" She swiped at her cheeks with the heel of her hand.

"How about I try to fix your water? In the meantime, but only if your mom allows, you get ready to go outside to say hi to Rosie and Briggs." He glanced up at Abby. "Let me show you the utility room."

He pulled off his old cowboy boots, hoping that Abby wouldn't notice that he still wore the same pair she had given him years ago. He'd tried to replace them, but somehow never found the right pair. Would she think he was still trying to hold on to the past?

"Could you keep an eye on this for me?" He took off his Stetson.

Charlotte's eyes grew big. "Can I try it on?"

"Of course," he laughed.

Her head disappeared inside the hat, and she giggled.

Charlotte stretched her arms in front of her and took a step.

"Take the hat off before you trip over something, please," Abby warned her daughter.

Charlotte lifted the hat. "Okay. I'll put it on my bed. So no one sits on it by accident."

Abby blew out a breath. "Okay."

Noah observed the exchange, determined not to get involved. Carrying the hat in both hands, Charlotte disappeared into her room.

He cleared his throat. "Shall we?"

"Give me a minute. I need to turn off the stove." Abby rushed off to the kitchen.

Charlotte skipped toward Noah and slipped her hand into his. "I set the table for us, come look."

His heart was turning to jelly. This girl had him wrapped around her little finger, and he was good with that.

She wiggled her index finger at him, then cupped her hands around her mouth. Noah bent down and leaned closer, ready to hear her secret.

"Mom wants you to stay," Charlotte whispered, then glanced toward the kitchen.

"Really?" he said under his breath.

"Yes, she made a lot of pancake batter. When it's just her and me, she only makes a little."

Noah suppressed a chuckle. "Thank you for telling me," he whispered back.

Charlotte placed her index finger over her lips.

Noah nodded. He would keep her secret. But what could he do if Abby asked him to leave? First things first—he strode toward the basement door and tugged at the doorknob.

"What's there?" Charlotte asked.

"The basement. I'll check on the water pump. Could you please tell your mom to come down so I can show her everything?"

"Sure." Charlotte zoomed away, and Noah turned on the light.

The old stairs creaked under his feet. He had not been down here in a while. There'd been no need—the space was mostly empty, and the few old boxes on the shelves weren't his. One day Abby would have to sort through the stuff left behind by her parents, but he was keenly aware that today was not the time to bring that up.

He opened the door to the utility room and pulled the chain

above his head. Dim light flooded the space. Noah took a permanent marker out of his pocket.

Electrical Panel, he wrote on the cover of the large metal box. Would she think him patronizing? Everyone knew what that was. Well, not everyone. And if Abby wasn't sure, how would she know where to shut off the power if she ever needed to?

Main Switch. He printed the letters on the face of the box and drew an arrow pointing to the large switch with a red handle. When he opened the panel, his suspicion was confirmed. This was an easy fix. The breaker for the pump circuit was off. Noah flicked it back on. The pump whirled. This should fix the problem. One more detail to take care of before he left. Noah leaned in, trying to read the faded script. It must have been Abby's dad who'd marked each switch.

"You fixed it?"

Abby's voice startled him. Her presence behind him sparked a million tiny tingles in his hands.

"It wasn't broken. The breaker was off. It may need to be replaced, but the pump is working now."

"Replaced?"

"These are all original. The house is, what, twenty-five years old? I know an electrician in town, Jim Tino."

"Jimmy?" Abby said, surprise in her voice.

"Yep, and he's pretty good. Do you want his number, or should I call him?"

"I can do that." The tone of her voice softened.

"Okay," he said and started to write next to each breaker.

"What are you doing?" Abby stood next to him and peered into the panel.

"The original labels are hard to read, and in case you ever need to shut something off or turn it back on, it'll be easier know which breaker is which."

Abby nodded.

He continued to write in large block letters. "Would you be okay if I wrote on the wall above the plug for the pump?"

"What?"

"If you ever need to shut off the water, you can just unplug it. No need to open the panel." He looked at the woman standing next to him. Suddenly, his stomach let out a loud growl. "Sorry, that was embarrassing." He chuckled.

A smile finally cracked on Abby's face. "Well, we have a big batch of pancake batter upstairs just waiting to be cooked up."

Warmth spread through his chest. And even though his stomach continued to rumble, he felt a jolt of joy. Abby had just invited him to breakfast. It was the first step in the right direction.

Chapter Eight

Back in the kitchen, Abby turned on the water. The faucet gurgled a little, and then a steady stream started to fill the sink. "Thank you," she said, while trying to shake off the claustrophobic feeling. Standing so close to Noah in the small utility room had made her uncomfortable. Their proximity seemed to stir up some long-forgotten feelings.

"You may need to give the batter another stir," she said to Charlotte. "And Noah is staying for breakfast, if that's okay with you." She smiled at her girl.

"Yay!"

Noah chuckled.

Charlotte took the whisk and tried to mix the thick batter. "It's stuck."

"Let's add a little milk." Noah came to the rescue. "Here." He splashed some in. "I'll start it for you, okay?"

She let go of the whisk handle.

"Thank you."

Noah pulled the utensil out of the sticky goop. "Let's loosen this up a little." A few stirs later, he handed the whisk back to Charlotte. "Your turn."

Abby put a piece of butter in the pan. She was thankful that Noah had taken the time to show her the mechanical parts of the house. Had she even known about the utility room? Her dad always took care of everything about the mechanics of the house, and she had no clue how anything worked. And Ken had hired people to do all that. There was no need for her to think about the electrical panel, the air-conditioning or the furnace.

Abby turned the stove back on. The butter in the frying pan began to melt.

"Who do I call to refill the propane tank?" she asked.

"The number is stamped on the tag attached to the tank, but I can give it to you as well. When I was living here, they came by every three months, but you may need to ask them to come more often."

"You lived here?" Charlotte stopped stirring.

"For a while."

"Did Rosie and Briggs live here, too?" Her little eyes sparkled.

"Yes," he replied attentively.

"So, they know this house?"

Abby knew where this was going.

"Charlotte, the pan is hot. Is the batter ready?"

"Yes, Mom." She brought the bowl to the stove. "Mommy, I think that Rosie and Briggs are lonely in the truck, don't you?"

"They are probably sleeping," Noah said.

"I don't think so." Charlotte sounded pretty sure. "They are excited to play with me and won't sleep. I can never sleep when I'm excited. Like at Christmas. Right, Mommy? I lay in bed, looking at the ceiling, thinking and thinking. I'm pretty sure they are looking at the door, thinking, 'Where's Charlotte? What is taking her so long?'"

Noah laughed.

But the torrent of words made Abby pause. Her little girl was talking. Nonstop. The way she used to. Abby picked up the batter and ladled a scoop onto the hot frying pan. Was this what Charlotte needed to recover from the divorce?

Glancing at her daughter, she saw her eyes were pleading with her.

"Okay." Abby bit her lip. "We can give it a try."

"Yes!" Charlotte hugged her so hard, it actually hurt.

"But only if Noah agrees, and the dogs behave," Abby added. She looked at him.

He grinned, spun on his heel and walked toward the door.

"Want to come?" He winked at Charlotte. "They'll be happy to see you."

Abby sighed. She wasn't ready for this. Not in the least bit.

Noah opened the truck's cab door, and the two excited Vizslas jumped out. They ran around them and stopped in front of Charlotte, their tails wagging with excitement.

"Can I pet them?"

"For sure." Noah laughed. "That's the only reason they come all the way up here."

"Where do they come from?"

"My apartment, of course."

Her eyes grew wide. "I've never been to an apartment."

Noah paused.

"We had a house, not an apartment. Before Dad moved to Florida." Charlotte scratched Briggs behind his ears. "He has a new house now. And a new family." She let out a long breath. Rosie butted in, and the girl used her other hand to give her some love, too. "My dad doesn't like me anymore."

What was he supposed to say to this little girl? Abby hadn't shared much about her failed marriage, and the last thing he wanted was to say things that would make the situation even worse.

"He likes his new baby now."

Briggs licked Charlotte's hand. This was his way of making things better. Dogs were so intuitive.

"I don't know about that, Charlotte. Do you think that a person can just stop liking someone?"

Her eyes were swimming with tears. "I miss Daddy."

Noah knelt and cautiously wrapped his arms around the little person in front of him, silently praying that Abby would be okay with that. He held the sobbing girl, unable to speak, as he didn't trust his voice not to betray the sorrow he felt for this child.

Rosie whined. Charlotte sniffed. "Is she okay?" she said between her sobs.

"I think she wants a hug, too," Noah said, struggling to smile.

Charlotte wiggled out of his embrace and wrapped her arms around Rosie's neck.

"I love you, Rosie. You're the nicest doggy ever." She kissed her on the wet nose. "And you, too." She stretched out her arm and pulled Briggs into a hug.

Noah cleared his throat. "Maybe we should go in, so your mom doesn't worry."

"Okay." Charlotte tried to peek into his truck.

"What are you looking for?"

"Their leashes."

Noah smiled. "Good call. We don't want them to think that the house is all theirs. Your mom might tell us that the visit is over before we can finish those yummy pancakes."

Charlotte used her sleeve to wipe the tears off her face.

"Please don't tell her I cried. It makes her sad when I do." She took one of the leashes from his hand and clicked it onto Rosie's collar. "And then she cries at night. She doesn't think I know, but I hear her. Come." She directed the dog toward the front door. Rosie eagerly followed.

Noah gently tugged at Briggs's leash and strode toward the house.

Lord help me out here, please. I've no clue what to do in this situation.

Chapter Nine

"Hey, you two. I was worried that we would be eating cold pancakes." Abby was setting down a jar of jam on the dining room table.

The dogs obediently stepped into the house.

"We're here. Look, Mom." Charlotte's voice was filled with enthusiasm. "Sit," she commanded Rosie. The dog obeyed, her eyes firmly fixed on the plate of steaming pancakes. "And you sit here." Charlotte pointed to the spot next to Rosie. Briggs obeyed.

"And where do I sit?" Noah asked, amusement in his voice.

"You can sit over there." Abby pointed to the far end of the table.

"Thanks." Noah pulled the chair out and sat down.

Charlotte sat in the chair next to him.

"But that's not your usual seat, honey." Abby pointed to the table setting next to her.

"Just for today, Mom," Charlotte pleaded. She gathered up the placemat, her plate and cutlery, and set everything next to Noah. That left Abby virtually alone at the other end of the table. Should she move closer to them?

"The pancakes sure smell good." Noah grinned at her daughter. Charlotte reached toward the center of the table and picked up the serving plate.

"For you, Noah. These are the best pancakes in the world."

"Maybe your mom should have some first," he said, glancing up at Abby.

"Oh, no, you go ahead." She waved him off. "There's plenty to go around."

"In that case, if you don't mind." Noah speared three pancakes in one swift move. "I'm starving. I didn't have much to eat during my shift last night at the vet clinic."

"So am I." Charlotte picked up her fork and served herself three pancakes as well.

"You'll eat all that?" Abby's eyebrows shot up.

"I'm starving, Mom."

"Well, that's good news." She reached for the serving plate and picked two pieces for herself. "There is mulberry jam, peanut butter and syrup. Help yourself, please." She glanced up at Noah.

"Thank you." He seemed to want to say something else but hesitated. Then he finally spoke.

"Do you have any coffee?"

"Oh, for sure," Abby said. "I brewed a fresh pot and forgot to bring it to the table."

"I can get it." He had popped out of his chair and was already walking toward the kitchen. Carafe in hand, he returned to the table and filled her cup.

"Let me get the cream," he said, setting the coffeepot down in front of her.

"It's right here." Abby reached for the pitcher and passed it to him. Their fingers touched, and she almost dropped the small ceramic container. Abby quickly looked away, hoping he had not noticed.

Noah took the cream out of her hand, picked up the coffeepot with the other and made his way back to the table. Sitting back in his chair, he poured himself a cup. After adding some cream, he took a sip.

She looked at him just as he glanced at her over the rim of his cup.

He caught her gaze.

Abby flushed, then looked down at her plate and started furiously cutting into the pancakes.

What had come over her? It was only breakfast. She had to try to get a hold of her emotions.

The coffee was nice and hot, but that wasn't the only reason for the warmth spreading through him. Abby's cheeks had turned pink when they'd looked at each other. Noah put down his mug and picked up a fork.

"Charlotte, could you pass me the peanut butter, please?"

"Sure," the girl said, her mouth full.

Thankfully, she seemed too busy spreading jam to notice anything out of the ordinary between him and her mother.

A low whine reminded everyone that there were more animals in the room than the three humans.

"Can they eat pancakes?" Charlotte asked, her eyes sparkling.

"Yes, but what they really want is the peanut butter. It's their favorite."

"Mine too." Charlotte reached for the jar and dunked her knife in it. She scooped a large chunk. "Can I give it to them?"

"That's kind of—"

"Don't feed them from the table," Abby interrupted.

"But they're hungry, Mom."

"Your mom is right," Noah said. "Why don't we finish breakfast first and then we can give them a little treat?"

"But what if they cry?"

"Then they'll have to go into the hallway," Abby said, and set her cutlery down. "If you want Briggs and Rosie to come into the house to play with you, we'll have to set some rules."

"For sure," Noah chimed in.

The dogs whined again, as if they sensed what they were talking about.

"Shhh," Charlotte said. "You heard what Mom said, and she's the boss."

Rosie grunted, then sprawled out next to Charlotte's chair. Briggs's eyes zeroed in on Charlotte's plate.

"You have to listen, too, or it'll be really lonely in the hallway," Charlotte said in a stern tone.

Noah chuckled. "You would make a great dog trainer."

Charlotte smiled as she put the last piece of pancake into her mouth. She chewed pensively, then looked up at Noah. "Where do they sleep at night?"

"They have beds."

"Like mine?"

"Nope, dog beds," Noah clarified. This girl was something else. Cute and smart. She definitely won his heart in the past two short days.

"Do they need blankets?"

"Nope."

"What about the puppies? Do they sleep with their mom and dad?"

"Actually, dogs are a bit different. Daddy dogs don't stay with the mom at first. Mommy dogs really don't like anyone near their babies. At least for the first few days."

Charlotte dropped her fork. She stared at him, tears welling up in her eyes.

Noah looked at Abby in desperation. What had he said to start this waterfall of tears?

"Oh, Charlotte." Abby was up on her feet, arms instantly wrapped around her daughter.

"I'm so sorry," Noah whispered.

Abby just shook her head and pulled her daughter close.

Noah exhaled, pushed his chair back and started to gather up the dishes from the table.

"Why don't you leave it?" Abby asked.

"I'm sorry. I didn't mean to…" Noah said as he continued to clear the table.

"I know. It's all right," Abby said.

"What else would you like me to do?"

"Maybe it would be best if you leave?"

Noah headed toward the kitchen and set the dirty dishes on the counter.

"Rosie, Briggs."

The dogs rushed to his side.

"But—" Charlotte gulped for breath. "But—"

"Here." He tore a piece of paper towel and gave it to the crying child.

"Thank you, Noah." She untangled herself from Abby's embrace and blew into the paper towel. "But I don't want you to go. You said I can play with the dogs." She stared at Abby through her tears.

"But if Noah makes you cry—"

"*He* doesn't make me cry." She let out a sob. "I just felt sorry for the puppies. If their daddy doesn't see them, they must miss him so much."

"That's not what I meant, honey." Noah stopped at the door. "Briggs would surely like to see his puppies, but Rosie will be very protective of the pups and won't allow anyone near them. All mommy dogs do that. Cats, too. Lots of animals, actually."

Charlotte sniffed. Abby stared at him.

"They love their babies so much that they often don't even get up to eat. Their owners have to make them go outside. But only for a few minutes, because the moms always run back and then lick their babies, just to let them know how much they love them." Noah met Abby's eyes, then walked toward the front door, shoved his feet into the well-worn boots and reached for his hat. He let his dogs out and stepped out of the cabin.

Abby stood in the middle of the dining room, staring at the

door. He was so kind to Charlotte. How was he to know that a simple mention of puppies would trigger her little girl? She glanced at Charlotte. New tears sprang up.

"What is it?"

"I don't want them to leave." She broke into a sprint, yanked the front door open and called the dogs at the top of her lungs. "Rosie! Briggs!"

"Charlotte," Abby called out to her, but her daughter kept running out the door.

"Noah, I'm sorry."

Abby rushed after her. When she walked out of the house, she halted. Noah was kneeling on the gravel, Charlotte's arms wrapped tightly around his neck. The two dogs were somehow part of this tangled embrace. Charlotte was sobbing into Noah's neck, and he was gently rubbing her back. Abby felt like an outsider. This was her daughter. She should be the one comforting her child. Abby walked slowly toward them.

"Charlotte," she said in a whisper. "I think Noah has to go now." Abby gently tugged at her daughter's T-shirt. Charlotte slowly released Noah from her embrace.

"Thank you for the hug," she whispered. "Can you come tomorrow? We may not have pancakes, but we can have toast, right, Mom?" She looked up and reached for Abby's hand.

Noah swallowed, then stood up. He looked at Abby, then back to Charlotte.

"How about I call your mom later this afternoon and see what you're both up to tomorrow?"

Abby wrapped her arms around Charlotte, then slowly nodded. Noah was clearly giving her an out, but she wouldn't lie to her daughter. Of course, they had nothing planned for tomorrow, or the day after, except cleaning and decluttering this old house.

"I'll call you," she said to Noah. "And thank you for coming. Maybe we can all go for a short walk tomorrow, so the dogs can run and get some exercise."

Charlotte threw her arms around Abby's waist. "You're the best mom in the whole world."

The tears instantly disappeared, and this happy child proclaimed her the mother of the year.

Noah just stared.

When Rosie let out a small bark, it seemed as if he returned from some faraway place.

"For sure, tomorrow would be fine. The dogs love it here. " He opened the truck door and let them jump in. "But I'd better go now. I need to get some sleep."

Noah pulled himself up into the truck, shut the door and rolled down his window.

"Thank you for the delicious breakfast. And you were right, those were the best pancakes I've ever had."

He shifted into Reverse, then turned around and drove his truck down the gravel driveway, back to civilization.

"All right," Abby said, tousling Charlotte's hair. "How about we attack those dishes and then see what needs to be done around here today?"

"Can we go to town, Mom?"

"Yes, but not today." Abby walked back to the house. She had no emotional energy left, and a trip to town might open old wounds of Noah's betrayal. Right now, she would stay put in this safe place her parents had left for her.

Driving down the mountain, Noah was unsure what to make of the entire situation. It was clear Abby needed his help, even though she would vehemently deny it. From what he had seen in that basement, he knew that the cabin would need some major updates. Noah had known that for a while, but as long as he'd lived there, the outdated systems never bothered him. He was used to fixing things around the property.

Now everything had changed.

And then there was little Charlotte. That sweet girl was dealing with a lot of sadness in her life right now. How could he help her?

Rosie whimpered, as if she had read his thoughts.

"I know, girl, you feel it, too." He reached back and patted each eager head in turn.

His phone rang. He pressed the button on his steering wheel. "Hey."

"Noah." Cindy's voice filled the cab. "Hope I didn't wake you, but I felt you needed to know."

"Haven't made it to bed yet. What's up?"

"Two things. The puppy food to mix in with Rosie's regular kibble just arrived."

"Great, I've been thinking about that. Time to switch her over."

"The second thing is…" She paused. "I called all the shelters and rescue facilities within a three-hour driving distance."

"Great. So, who's picking up the puppy?"

"That's why I'm calling. No one has space."

"What?"

"Everyone says the same thing. They're short-staffed. The best response I got was from Boulder, but they said we have to wait two months before they can take the pup."

"Two months? We can't keep it at the clinic for two months."

"Yeah, Dr. Gina said the same thing."

"And?"

"She said to ask you if you could take it."

"Me?"

"Yep."

He hadn't told his coworkers about the move to the condo. There was no need to reveal every detail of his personal life to the clinic staff. But taking the puppy to his apartment was out of the question. He would have to talk to Gina.

"Okay, I'll call her later today after I get some sleep. I'm too tired to negotiate something like this right now."

"For sure. See you tonight." Cindy hung up the phone.

Noah parked in his designated spot, hopped out of the truck and put the dogs on their leashes. He led them down the street, away from the grassy area in front of the apartment building.

"Time for a little walk, and then we've got to get some shut-eye."

On the way back to his apartment, he looked toward the mountains. The scenery filled his heart with joy. Maybe he should call his real estate agent and start looking for a cabin. At first, he'd decided against it, and that's why he got stuck with this terrible condo. He didn't want to live like a hermit any longer. Staying at the cabin, paying minimal rent, had helped him to save up for his place, but as much as he loved the woods, he'd also felt isolated and lonely. Working at the clinic was his only means of escape, but returning to the empty cabin every night had made his heart heavy. That's why he had gotten his two amazing dogs three years before. They were so in tune with his feelings. The unconditional love they gave so freely almost made his loneliness bearable.

Noah pushed open the door to his building and stepped into the hallway. Thankfully, Brenda was nowhere to be seen.

He took the steps two at a time, unlocked his condo and shut the door firmly behind him and his two faithful companions.

This was his sanctuary. His place of refuge. His home. Yet it felt as cold as an iceberg. He could get more furniture, a couple of rugs and a new set of dishes. But none of that would change the way he felt.

He sank into the sofa. Exhaustion kicked in. Noah managed to reach for a blanket. The dogs recognized the familiar signal and took up their assigned positions, with Rosie at his feet and Briggs wriggling at Noah's side.

God, this can't be all there is to life.

Before he could finish the prayer with an amen, he was asleep.

Chapter Ten

Finally, Saturday arrived. The moment Charlotte woke up she buzzed with excitement. They were going to town. Abby checked her purse. She had her phone, wallet and car keys. The list was there, too. Her and Charlotte would have an entire day to themselves, doing what Saturdays were meant for—shopping.

Calling Noah yesterday had been way outside her comfort zone. He'd agreed to postpone today's visit to the cabin until tomorrow after church. Right now, she had an excited girl prancing around the house. The plan was to drive to town for a little shopping trip. The only thing Abby worried about was her daughter's disappointment once she realized that there wasn't an actual mall in town.

"Charlotte, are you ready?"

This would be the first trip down the mountain to the small town of Hope Rock since they had arrived at the house. Abby hesitated. Was she ready for it? What if she saw *her*? The thought of running into Natalie, her former best friend—and Noah's brother's high school girlfriend—after all these years still gave her anxiety. Abby blamed her for her breakup with Noah and all the heartache that followed. The prom night heartbreak had happened a lifetime ago. It was more than time to let it go. She had moved on, built a new life in a city, married Ken and had an amazing daughter. And despite her marriage not working out, she didn't see herself as a failure—most days.

"I'm ready!" Charlotte ran into the hallway, took a leap and landed right in front of Abby.

"Great!" Abby said, happy that her girl was getting her spirit back.

"I made a shopping list, Mom."

"Let me see it, to make sure that we don't double up on things."

Charlotte pulled a carefully folded sheet of lined paper from her back pocket, clutching her favorite crayon in the other hand. Abby opened it. It was decorated with hand-drawn pictures of two dogs, a bunch of puppies and three stick-figure people. Abby felt a sense of pride in her heart as she read Charlotte's carefully printed pink letters.

1. Pink dog bowl
2. Blue dog bowl
3. 10 small dog bowls, 5 pink and 5 blue
4. Slippers for Noah
5. Chocolate for Mom
6. Pink stuff for me

Abby smiled widely.

"Do you think Noah needs slippers?"

"He walks around here in socks and winter is coming," Charlotte chimed, slipping into her windbreaker.

"It's only August." Abby opened the door. A gust of wind blew into the house. Did her daughter think Noah would become a permanent fixture around here?

"Yep, but it'll snow before you know it." Charlotte walked through the door.

"And what about all the dog stuff?" Abby unlocked the car and they both got in. "Ten little bowls?"

"I want to be ready."

"Ready for what?" Abby started the engine.

Charlotte settled in and buckled herself into her booster seat. "For the puppies!"

She would have to address this right away so Charlotte wouldn't get her hopes up. "But they're Noah's puppies. What makes you think they'll need bowls at our house?"

"When they come to visit with their mommy and daddy, of course."

Abby had to admit that having the dogs around was beneficial for Charlotte. But having twelve dogs running through the cabin was totally out of the question. She would need to discuss this with Noah, in case he was thinking the same as Charlotte. The two dogs were trouble enough, although she had to admit they were well behaved. She glanced at her daughter.

"What are you writing?" Abby asked as she glanced in her rearview mirror.

"I'm making a new list."

"School supplies?"

"No." The girl frowned. "Puppy names."

"Puppy names? Did Noah ask you to do that?"

"No, but I've decided he'll definitely need some help. Who can come up with so many awesome dog names right as they're being born?"

Abby chuckled. "You have a point."

"I know."

Well, her confidence was returning. Hadn't Abby prayed for that?

"Buckled?" Abby checked as she tossed her pink purse on the passenger seat.

"Yes, Mom." Charlotte let out a dramatic sigh, like a teenage girl, even though she was only six.

Abby suppressed a smile. The seat belt clicked and her daughter turned toward her.

"I'm so excited, I can't wait."

"I see that." Abby chuckled and started the engine. She drove down the driveway, her heart filling with peaceful gratitude. She and Charlotte would be okay. The smile on her daughter's face assured her of that.

They passed the sign that said Welcome to Hope Rock. Abby gripped the steering wheel a little tighter. It had been over a decade since she had driven down Main Street. A lot had changed. Large planters filled with blooming flowers lined both sides of the road. Most of the stores looked new. Had she driven through town on a road trip, there was a chance she wouldn't even recognize it. Then, a smile crossed her face. Rocco's Pizza was still there, looking exactly the same as it had during her high school days. How many Sunday evenings had she spent in their favorite booth, sharing a pizza with Noah, talking about their future after graduation? Perhaps she should take Charlotte there for lunch after they had finished shopping.

They found a parking spot in front of the Everything Mart. Charlotte unbuckled herself and hopped out of the car, then carefully folded her shopping list and tucked it into her back pocket.

"I'll get the cart!" Excited, she zoomed across the parking lot without looking.

"Charlotte!" Abby's heart almost stopped. Thankfully, no cars were coming from either direction. With a few quick strides, she reached her daughter.

"Don't run off like that. It's dangerous."

"But I did look."

The tears were streaming down her daughter's face. Abby knew she had to stop this before it ruined the entire morning. She squatted down, then wrapped her arms around her daughter.

"I can't even think of what I would do if something happened to you, sweetheart."

Charlotte gave her a tight squeeze. When she slowly pulled out of her embrace a few seconds later, she looked her in the eyes.

"Mom, you don't have to be scared. I won't leave you like Dad. Ever. I promise."

Abby gulped as tremors rose from somewhere in her core and rapidly spread through her entire body. She stood up and reached for a shopping cart. It was stuck. Her shaking hands gave her away to Charlotte, to the store, to the entire world. The last thing Abby wanted was to put this burden on her child. Charlotte wasn't her therapist or a supportive friend. She was her six-year-old daughter.

Abby tugged at the stuck shopping cart one more time. The thing finally released. She filled her lungs with a shaky breath, suppressed her tears and commanded her hands to stop shaking. She wouldn't fall apart in front of a store, with Charlotte watching her.

"I know, sweetheart," Abby said and reached for the small hand. "And I promise I won't ever leave you. Because you and I have each other, and that will never change. You and me against the world."

"And Noah," Charlotte chimed in, "and Rosie and Briggs. And soon there will be more of us against the whole world. Just wait till all the puppies get here. It will be so good—you'll see, Mommy. I can't wait."

Abby gripped Charlotte's hand a little tighter and forced herself to take a deep breath. She struggled to fill her lungs. Her heart rate sped up with every step that brought her closer to the store. They would go inside, get all the items on their lists, maybe minus the dog stuff, and walk back to their car.

"Are you okay, Mom?" a little voice chirped.

"Yes. Why?"

"You're squeezing my hand really hard."

"Oh, I'm so sorry, sweetheart." Abby released her grip. "Just hold on to the cart."

"Do I have to? I'm not a baby."

"Only till we get inside. Then you can let go."

"How about we get a snack before we get to the fun part?" Abby forced a smile into her voice.

"Can I get a hot chocolate with whipped cream?"

"If they have it, sure."

Charlotte skipped. And at that moment, Abby wished for the same kind of lightness.

The automated door swished open and they walked in. This store was new. Abby recalled that years ago, there used to be an old feed store in this spot.

"The coffee is over there." Charlotte sped up ahead of her.

"Stay with me."

"But Mom—"

Abby scanned the store.

"Please," she whispered, not wanting to embarrass herself or her daughter. There was no one lurking along the walk from the front door to the coffee area to snatch her kid. She forced herself to take a breath, counted to five, then exhaled slowly. She leaned on the counter, contemplating whether she should go full or only half sweet. It would be her first pumpkin spice latte of the season. The sugar might give her a boost of energy she so desperately needed.

"Can I get some pumpkin in my drink, too, Mommy?" Charlotte tugged at her sleeve.

"Sure, honey." Abby tried to smile. Her stomach tightened. The sweet scent of the flavored syrups suddenly made her nauseous.

They placed the order and Abby pushed the shopping cart toward a small table for two. She needed to sit down and get a grip on this *thing* that kept clinging to her like a spiderweb. To be free of this underlying anxiety would be such an answer to prayer. It had been less than a week since she'd been back in the mountains, her plans for updating the house barely started, yet she felt drained. The exhaustion didn't go away, even though she had slept better the past two nights. If she fell ill, who would take care of Charlotte?

Just then, the barista called out their names.

Abby got up, picked up their drinks and turned back to their table. A crayon tapping at her bottom lip, her girl was in deep thought, her list spread before her.

"What are you thinking about?" Abby asked.

"The puppy names for Noah."

Abby smiled at her daughter, who was so kind and thoughtful that she'd come up with dog names for someone she barely knew.

"Cookie," Charlotte blurted out. "What do you think, Mom?"

"I like Cookie."

"Because you love cookies!" Charlotte giggled. "Could I get one?"

"Sure."

"Can I buy it myself?"

"Here." Abby gave her a five-dollar bill. "Make sure you wait for the change."

"I know, Mom."

After a few minutes, Charlotte came back to the table. "Here's yours, Mom," she said, handing her a paper bag.

"Thank you. And the change?"

"Here," Charlotte said, placing the coins right next to the list.

"How do you know Rosie is having ten puppies? Did Noah tell you?"

"No."

"So, how do you know?"

"God told me."

Abby's eyebrows shot up. "*God* told you? What do you mean?"

"I prayed for Rosie to be a good mommy, and then I wanted to know how many times I needed to pray so that she would be a good mommy to each puppy. So, I asked God how many she had in her tummy." Charlotte took a bite of her cookie.

"Did God tell you anything else?" Abby asked her as she sipped her latte.

"Yep." Charlotte licked the whipped cream off the top of

her hot chocolate. "Not to get any collars for the pups, because Noah is getting them."

Abby's fingers still shook a bit as she took the lid off her coffee cup. Charlotte's colorful imagination was on its way back from wherever it had been hiding for the past several weeks. That made her happy. If only she could will away this panic attack, her life would be as close to normal as she dared to hope.

"And to get him the slippers," Charlotte added before stuffing the last piece of the cookie into her mouth.

"All right, in that case," Abby said, trying to sound cheerful, "we better finish up here and get going. We have pink stuff, dog dishes and Noah's slippers to buy."

"Yep." Charlotte picked up her empty paper cup. "Size twelve and a half." She beamed. "I peeked at his boots when you were talking in the basement."

Abby bit her lip to keep from laughing as her daughter marched toward the garbage can, tossed in her used cup and spun around, the cutest smile ever on her face. Then Abby stood up and reached for the empty chair next to her. But the world started spinning.

And everything went black.

The ringing of his phone woke Noah up. He looked around, slightly disoriented. Last night at the clinic was so busy that he hadn't stopped for a second. Not even to call Abby and check on them. He had not seen them since Wednesday. Rosie and Briggs stirred on the bed. He sat up and looked around his bedroom. Noah rubbed his hand across the back of his neck, trying to get the kink out.

The phone rang again. Noah glanced at his nightstand. It was empty. He must have left it in the hallway. With a few long strides, the gadget was in his hand.

"Abby?" he responded.

"No, it's Charlotte."

"Charlotte? Is everything okay?"

"No."

Her sobs sent chills down his arms.

"Are you okay?" he asked her.

"Yes. But Mom—"

"Charlotte, where are you?"

"At the big store. We went to get you slippers and bowls for the puppies and Mommy—"

Another sob.

"Take a deep breath and tell me slowly what's going on." He reached for his jeans and T-shirt.

"Mommy fainted. The lady who works here is helping her. She asked me to call my dad, but I—"

"Shhh, that's okay," Noah reassured her as he grabbed his truck keys. "I'm on my way."

"—don't have his number."

"It was good that you called me." Noah shoved his feet into his old boots. Locking the door behind him, he ran down the stairs. "I'm getting into my truck now and will be there in five minutes. Where's your mom?"

"The lady took us to the office. She's on the folding bed right next to me."

"Can I speak to her?"

"Mommy? Noah wants to talk to you. She isn't talking." Charlotte's voice broke.

"Is the lady there?"

"She's on the phone."

"Okay, as soon as she hangs up, give her your mom's phone. I need to talk to her. I'm four minutes away, sweetheart. You're doing great."

"Noah, I'm scared."

"And that's okay. We can only be brave when we're scared, and you're being super brave right now."

"I don't feel brave," she cried into the phone.

"Two minutes and I'm there." Noah turned into the store's parking lot. "You're at the big store, right?"

"Yes. Can you hurry?"

An ambulance siren blared behind his truck. Noah parked, jumped out of the cab and ran into the store.

"Which way to the office?" he asked the first employee he saw. The startled teenager pointed past the coffee area.

"Thanks."

His heart pounded in his ears. What had happened to Abby? Was she still unconscious? The siren grew louder, then shut off, leaving the swirling blue light flashing through the front windows of the store.

"Charlotte," he called out and reached for the crying girl. Noah wrapped his arms around her and held her tight. Her little fingers dug into his back.

"Is she going to be okay?" she asked through her tears.

"The paramedics are here. They'll take good care of her." Noah glanced at Abby. Her pale face barely registered his presence.

"Excuse us," said the first responder as she stepped into the room. She set the stretcher down, leaning it against the narrow wall. "We'll need some space to work." Her partner's deep voice filled the office.

"Come on." Noah let go of the distraught girl. "Let's wait in the hallway so that they can take care of your mom."

Charlotte squeezed his hand and let out a ragged breath.

"Are you okay?" Noah ran the back of his hand down her wet cheek.

She nodded and then followed him out of the office.

"She just fainted," said the middle-aged woman leaning on the wall opposite. "I had just given her a coffee. Nothing was wrong with it. The milk was fresh."

Noah glanced at her. The woman's face was flushed.

"I don't think it has anything to do with the latte, ma'am. Thank you for taking care of her and calling 911."

"How long was she unconscious?" one of the paramedics called out from the room.

"Only a few minutes. She came to as I tried to help her walk to the office."

The uniformed man called out a string of orders; his calm voice carried urgency. His partner unzipped a duffel bag and passed him a blood pressure cuff.

"Ma'am," the first responder said loudly. He must have been trying to get Abby's attention.

"Ma'am?"

The female paramedic stepped into the hallway. "Are you the husband?"

"No, but—"

"He's Mr. Noah," Charlotte chimed in.

"Okay," the woman said, looking at Charlotte. "And who are you?"

"Charlotte is Abby's daughter. Abby and I are friends."

The woman nodded. "Any medical conditions you know of?"

"No. But she has been under a tremendous amount of stress lately."

"Is your mom taking any medicine?"

"Only when she gets a headache."

"How often does she have those? Every day? Once a week?"

"Not every day," Charlotte replied, her voice still quivering.

"Some assistance here," the male paramedic called from the office.

"On it." The woman immediately joined her colleague.

"How about we get another hot chocolate while the paramedics check your mom and find out what's going on?" Noah tried to disguise his worry, but he was sure he had failed.

Charlotte gripped his hand. "I want to stay near Mommy."

"They'll come and get us, I'm sure."

"What if they take her away?"

Noah hadn't thought of that. What would happen to Charlotte if Abby had to be admitted to the hospital?

"I tell you what. The coffee shop is right by the entrance, so if they decide your mom needs a better checkup at the hospital, they will have to pass by us, because that's the only door and their ambulance is parked right outside."

"Okay." Charlotte's voice was so fear-filled that it broke Noah's heart.

"She'll be fine." He patted her back gently. He had no idea what was going on with Abby, but panicking the girl would only make the situation worse.

They walked hand in hand to the coffee counter. Noah sat Charlotte down so that she could see the front door.

"Wait here, I'll get our hot chocolates."

A silent nod, tears still streaming down her face.

Noah placed the order and picked up a wad of napkins. He handed them to Charlotte and watched her wipe her face and blow her nose.

With two cups in hand, he sat next to her.

"Here, try taking a sip. But be careful, it's pretty hot."

She brought the cup to her lips. Charlotte blew on the frothy milk, then dipped in her tongue. "Thank you," she whispered and then took a sip.

Noah cleared his throat. "Charlotte, the doctor might need to ask you a few questions. Has this ever happened before to your mom?"

"No."

"Did your mom say that she didn't feel well when you got up this morning?"

Charlotte shook her head.

"Did she feel ill driving to the store?"

"Nope."

"Can you think of anything that could help the doctor figure out what went wrong?"

"She was breathing funny."

"What do you mean?"

"When she got the shopping cart, I asked her if she was okay. She said she was. Then we came inside and—"

Charlotte struggled to keep the tears at bay.

"You're doing great." Noah patted her hand.

"Mom!" The girl sprang to her feet.

The two paramedics were wheeling out the stretcher. Abby was strapped to it.

"Charlotte." He got up and rushed after the girl. "Wait!"

"We need to run some more tests, so we'll be taking her with us," said the female first responder.

"Okay." Noah reached for Charlotte and wrapped his arm around her shaking shoulders.

Abby opened her eyes.

"I'll take Charlotte to the hospital in my truck, is that okay?"

Abby nodded, then motioned toward her purse, sitting atop the blanket.

The automated door swooshed open. The gurney rolled out of the store and Noah followed, firmly holding Charlotte's hand.

The paramedics pushed the gurney into the ambulance. One of them handed Noah Abby's purse.

"She wants you to take it," said the man in a deep baritone.

"Thank you," Noah said, taking the bag from his hand.

As soon as the paramedic was back inside, his partner firmly shut the door and rushed toward the driver's side.

"Let's get into my truck," Noah urged Charlotte.

"Are Rosie and Briggs there?"

"No, they're at home. Probably sleeping." Noah opened the passenger door and helped Charlotte climb in. He stretched the seat belt and clicked it in, then set Abby's purse on her lap. "Can you hold it?"

Charlotte nodded.

Noah frowned. "I may need to get you a booster seat."

"It's in Mom's car."

"Can you get her car keys from the purse?"

Charlotte glanced at the bag resting on her lap. "I'm not allowed."

"You're not allowed what?"

"Not allowed to go in her purse."

"This is an emergency. There are different rules for such a situation. Like getting the car keys from her bag, or using her phone like you did, which was really brave of you."

Charlotte shook her head and passed him the purse.

"I don't know about this."

"But you're her friend. And you won't get in trouble. She can't ground you."

Abby could do far worse than ground him, but the sad girl in front of him didn't need to know all about that.

"You're right," Noah sighed. "Why don't you open it and I'll see if I can fish out the keys."

Charlotte nodded visibly relieved.

Noah's hand dove in.

Rummaging through a woman's purse was completely out of his comfort zone. His fingers found a wallet and a case for her sunglasses.

There, all the way to the bottom, his fingers brushed a plastic car key.

"Got it." Noah took it out and blew out a breath. "Give me a minute, I'll go get the booster seat from your mom's car."

Noah paused. Leaving his dogs in the truck was one thing. No reasonable person would get near. The friendly Vizsla would turn into a fiercely protective mother of the pack and bark her head off. Charlotte, on the other hand—

"Why don't you come with me?" Noah asked Charlotte. "And take anything that you might need out of the car. I'll figure out if we can leave it parked here till your mom gets better, or if I need to ask someone to help me bring it up to the cabin."

The girl nodded and unclicked her seat belt, then reached for his hand and hopped out of the truck.

Her fingers wrapped around his, but if anyone could see inside him, they would see that little hand reached all the way inside his chest and held his heart. Noah smiled at the little girl.

"Hey, you and me…we got this."

She bit her lip, then nodded.

"We'll get that seat and then drive to the hospital to see your mom, kiddo."

Noah hoped they'd get good news when they arrived. Surely Abby would be ready to go home, because he had no idea how to become an instant dad to this little girl.

Noah cleared his throat and pressed the key fob. Abby's car flashed its lights four parking spots to the left.

He exhaled a sigh of relief. "Okay, let's get your stuff and be on our way."

Chapter Eleven

Noah parked in the lot nearest to the emergency room entrance and helped Charlotte hop out of the truck. She swung Abby's purse over her shoulder, as if it belonged to her, then gripped his hand. Together, they walked through the automatic door into the triage area.

"We're here to see Abby Clifford. She was brought in a few minutes ago in an ambulance."

The nurse glanced at Charlotte.

"Let me check." She smiled at the little girl, most likely knowing how frightening the entire situation must be to a child. After a quick glance at her monitor, a slight frown came over her face. Then her professional smile returned as she looked at Charlotte again.

"Why don't you take a seat on the orange chairs, right over there. I'll come and get you when I have more information."

"Thank you." Noah nodded. Charlotte followed him.

"Would you like something to drink?" he asked her.

She shook her head.

"Are you hungry?"

Another shake.

Then Charlotte whispered, "I need to go to the bathroom."

"Okay." Noah got up and scanned the waiting room. "It's over there." He pointed to the left.

She stood and then glanced at him.

It took him a moment to realize that the girl expected him to go with her.

"Okay."

She grabbed his hand again.

It made him feel good. He was helping to make a bad situation a little better for this child.

They walked over to the door to the restroom.

"You'll have to go in by yourself," he said quietly.

Her big eyes met his.

"Mom always comes with me to make sure I'm okay."

"Well, I can't go with you in there. It's a girls' bathroom. Right?"

Charlotte bit her lip.

"You'll be fine. You must have used the bathroom at your school once or twice." He smiled at her. "Right?"

She nodded.

"It's just like that. I'll wait here, and if you need anything or feel unsafe, you call out and I will get one of the nurses to come in and help you. Okay?"

"Can you pray?"

"What?"

"When Mom and I pray, it helps me to be less afraid."

Noah had no problems with praying in front of people, but he had never talked to God in front of a public restroom. Almost everyone was on their phone, paying no attention to him or Charlotte.

"Dear God, please help Charlotte to be brave and keep her safe in the bathroom."

"Thanks." She grinned at him, pulled her hand out of his and pushed at the door. "Hold this." She pushed the bag toward him.

This girl was something else. He glanced at the purse and chuckled. How did he end up standing in front of the ladies' bathroom holding a pink purse? Out of the corner of his eye, he noticed the triage nurse get up from her desk and walk in the direction of the orange chairs. She looked around. Noah raised his arm, but she had not noticed him. He clenched the handle of the bag, fighting the urge to rush toward the woman.

He glanced at the bathroom door. But he couldn't leave Charlotte, even though he would be only a few steps away. Noah had promised he would wait, and breaking his word would undermine their trust.

A glance at his phone confirmed that the girl had been in the bathroom for only six minutes.

Please give me patience.

Suddenly, the door flew open and Charlotte stood in front of him.

"All done," she announced loud enough for the entire waiting room to hear.

Was he supposed to tell her she was a good girl, just as he did every time Rosie did her business?

"Great. The nurse was looking for us," he said and handed her back Abby's purse.

"Let's go. Hurry." Charlotte grabbed his hand and practically dragged him toward the triage station. "Is my mom okay?" the girl blurted before Noah had a chance to address the nurse.

The woman looked up from her monitor.

"Here you are. I can take you to see your mom now, if you like."

"Yes, please. I've got her purse and she might need it." Charlotte turned so the nurse could see the pink bag slung over her shoulder.

"I see." The nurse smiled. "Follow me, please."

Hand in hand, Noah and Charlotte walked through a set of doors that opened only with a staff card. The large room was divided into smaller spaces by a row of floor-to-ceiling curtains. The nurse stopped at the third one on their left and peeked in.

"Here she is," she said, looking at Charlotte. "You can go right in."

The curtain slid back on the overhead rail, and Noah followed the girl into the tiny space.

Abby was hooked up to a monitor with an IV line in her hand. Her eyes fluttered open.

"Charlotte." Abby tried to reach for her daughter. She sucked in her breath as the line pulled at her arm.

"Take it easy." Noah stepped closer.

"What are *you* doing here?"

"Noah drove me in his truck, Mom, and we got the booster seat out of your car."

Abby looked at her, puzzled.

"Noah found your car keys in your purse."

"My purse?"

"It's right here." Charlotte took it off her shoulder. "I brought it for you." She dumped the bag onto Abby's legs.

"What did the doctor say?" Noah asked.

Abby slowly turned her face toward him.

"You?"

Was she struggling to recognize him? Had she hit her head when she fainted, or had they given her some sedatives and the medication confused her?

The curtain pulled back, and a physician stepped into the crowded space.

"Hi, I'm Dr. James, and you are?"

"This is Abby's daughter, Charlotte, and I'm Noah, a longtime family friend."

"Not a relative?"

"No."

"Hmm, that puts me in a difficult situation. I can't share her medical information with you without her consent, but the paramedics had to give her a mild sedative, so she's unable to sign any paperwork." The doctor held Noah's gaze, then he glanced at Charlotte. "I tell you what. I will most likely be keeping Abby overnight. Given the lack of medical history—"

Noah motioned toward Charlotte, who stood right next to Abby's bed, holding her hand.

The doctor nodded as a silent understanding passed between them.

"Abby's parents passed away several years ago, and she's recently divorced. You can put my name down as an emergency contact. Charlotte will be staying with me for the duration of her mother's hospital stay."

Noah recited his cell number, and Dr. James wrote it on Abby's chart.

"Charlotte, why don't we let your mom rest? Dr. James will call us when she feels better so we can come see her." He reached for the girl's hand.

Her little fingers intertwined with his, and Noah wished he could be much more than an emergency contact to both of them.

Her teary eyes met his.

"Don't worry," Dr. James said, his voice reassuring. "We'll take very good care of your mother."

A lonely tear slid down Charlotte's cheek.

"Thank you, Dr. James." Noah gently pulled Charlotte closer and rested both of his hands on her shoulders. "Please call us as soon as she improves."

Chapter Twelve

Noah sat in his truck, with Charlotte next to him, buckled in the passenger seat in her booster. The girl seemed so sad, his heart was breaking for her. He couldn't have even imagined what was going through her mind. She must be so scared, still reeling from her parents' divorce, now her mom was in the hospital.

"Why don't we stop in town for pizza and make a plan?" he said, trying to sound cheerful.

"A plan?"

"From what the doctor said, your mom will have to stay overnight. So, you and I need to sort out a sleepover."

Her eyes grew big despite her sadness.

Thankfully, it was Saturday and he didn't have to go to work at the clinic tonight.

"Can I stay at your apartment?" Charlotte chimed.

"That might not work," he said and backed out of the parking lot. "I only have one bed and a sofa. Also, there are boxes everywhere and not much to eat in the fridge." He turned down Main Street. "I hope you like pizza," he said, glancing at his little passenger.

A smile lit up her face.

"Good. I don't need to pack much, aside from the dogs. I think it would be easier if we take them to your place. That way, if your mom needs anything, we can pack it for her and drive to the hospital."

"I would love to have a sleepover with Rosie and Briggs. Can they sleep in my bed?"

Noah filled his lungs and held his breath. That would be fine and dandy; the dogs usually shared the sofa with him and, on occasion, sneaked into his bed. But what would Abby say?

He pulled up in front of Rocco's Pizza and turned off his truck's engine.

"Let's talk about it inside."

Charlotte unbuckled herself but waited for him to walk around the truck and open the door for her. Noah picked the girl up and set her next to him on the sidewalk. He locked the car and she automatically reached for his hand.

They both walked into the pizza place. The aroma of freshly baked pizza instantly greeted them.

"I'm so hungry," Charlotte said enthusiastically.

The hostess grabbed two menus and led them to a booth by the window.

"Do you have any allergies?" He looked at Charlotte over his menu. His heart squeezed, watching the little girl struggling to be brave.

"I don't. Do you like pineapple on your pizza?"

"I sure do." He shot her a smile. "A large Hawaiian pie, it is."

Charlotte smiled back at him.

Abby woke up disoriented. The smell of disinfectant jarred her. Was she at a hospital? And where was her daughter? She reached for the call button and pressed it repeatedly, the heart monitor tracking her speeding pulse.

A nurse rushed into her room. "What's the—"

"Where is my daughter?" Abby blurted out.

"You need to calm down, ma'am. Your blood pressure is too high." The nurse rushed to the monitor and turned off the beeping alarm. "Your friend Noah took her home."

"Noah?" Abby tried to sit up, but the maze of IV lines attached to her body prevented her from doing so.

"I've got his number at the nurses' station. Would you like me to call him to let him know that you're awake?" Her gaze was soft, filled with care.

"When did I get here?" Abby leaned into the pillows.

"This morning."

"What happened? The last thing I remember is being at the store with my daughter."

"Let me call your attending physician so that you can discuss your test results with him." She gave her a reassuring smile.

Abby looked at her arm. A large square of tape secured an IV needle, dripping fluids into her vein. What was going on? She searched around for her phone and then carefully reached for the small drawer on her nightstand. Her fingers wrapped around her gadget and she exhaled with relief. Tapping the screen, Abby waited impatiently for Noah to pick up.

"Hey there," he answered, his voice sounding genuinely happy. "You're awake."

"Is that Mommy?"

Abby's eyes misted when she heard Charlotte's voice in the background. She was safe with him.

"Give me a second," he said. Abby listened to the muffled sounds as Noah talked to her daughter. "I'll be right over there, watching you, as you finish your slice."

"And then I'll get a turn?"

Tears welled up in Abby's eyes.

"Of course," she heard Noah say.

His tone was so kind—Abby's fingers tightened around her phone. How could she ever thank him for this? He'd come through for her when she and Charlotte needed him the most. This was Noah, whom she'd loved all those years ago.

A moment later, Noah's voice became clear once again.

"How are you?"

"Okay."

"What did the doctor say?"

"The nurse just went to get him."

"Are you still in the emergency room?"

"No, they must have transferred me while I slept."

"Good. How are you feeling?"

"Like I got run over by a truck. Can you tell me what happened?"

"Apparently, you fainted at the store. The staff called an ambulance and I picked up Charlotte. We're having pizza—"

"I don't think they'll let me go home today, Noah," Abby interrupted, her voice full of worry.

"I got that covered." His tone was calm and confident. "Charlotte and I are stopping at my condo. We'll pick up the dogs, and we'll go up to your house and stay there. Hope that's okay with you."

"Of course. How will I ever thank you?"

"Thank me?" He chuckled. "Charlotte is great. We'll have fun tonight, you get better and we'll sort out everything tomorrow morning."

"Thank you," she whispered.

"Abby—" he said, his voice filled with care.

A lump rose in her throat. She couldn't go there. Noah was a friend, and any feelings she'd had for him were somewhere in the past. And they needed to stay there.

"Thank you," she said. "I'll find a way to make it up to you."

"No need," he said, his voice husky.

A knock at the door cut into her conversation. The doctor walked into her room.

"I've got to go," she said quickly. "Tell Charlotte I'll call her back as soon as I can."

"Sure," he replied, with a hint of disappointment in his voice. "I'll tell her."

Abby disconnected the call and set the phone aside.

"I've got good news and bad news," Dr. James said, looking straight at her. "Which one would you like first?"

Abby took a deep breath, unsure she could handle anything unpleasant at the moment.

"Give me the good one. Please."

"Your bloodwork came back. You have been dehydrated, but with an IV drip, that'll be fine. Your oxygen levels are improving, and everything else seems to check out."

"Great." A little smile cracked her lips. She wasn't dying of some terrible disease. "So, what's the bad news?"

"Well—" He pushed his glasses back with his right index finger. "Since we don't know yet what exactly caused the blackout, by law, your driver's license will be automatically suspended—temporarily."

"What?" A swarm of thoughts instantly whirled in her head. Had she stayed in the city, this news wouldn't have been as devastating, but high up in the mountains? The school year was starting in a few weeks. How would she get groceries? What if something happened to Charlotte and she needed to take her to a doctor?

"But I need—"

"I understand." The doctor held her gaze. "There's more."

Abby gripped the bedsheet. What more could there be?

"You live alone." He flipped through her chart. "With a young daughter, correct?"

"Yes," her voice trembled.

"I need to inform local child services, so they can check on you from time to time, just to make sure all is—"

"What? Why? I was perfectly fine till this morning. Maybe my sugar was low."

"It wasn't."

Abby stared at him. Social services? Was he serious? What if the social worker decided that she was unfit to care for Charlotte?

"Are you telling me you have no idea what could have caused the fainting, Doctor?" Maybe if he ran a few more tests, this entire situation could be resolved with a simple prescription. "I've been under a lot of pressure lately and I struggle with anxiety."

"I see." He scribbled on the chart.

"And I can tell you that having social services monitor me like I'm a bad parent unable to care for my daughter will only exacerbate the issue." She glanced at the monitor. Her heart rate was elevated, and so was her blood pressure.

"No one is suggesting that you're a bad parent, Abby." He stuck the pen into his chest pocket. "But I'm obligated by law to report this."

"Is there anything else that can be done?" She hated the desperation in her voice.

The doctor held her gaze. "Do you know anyone in Hope Rock who could stay with you for a couple of weeks while we run follow-up tests and sort this out?"

How could she tell him she knew no one in town except Noah? And that he was the last person she wanted to stay at her house and babysit her?

"Maybe," she said under her breath.

"Could you contact that person? And if he or she agrees to stay with you, I won't file the forms for the home visits."

Her eyes filled with tears. Abby reached for a tissue. How could she ask Noah to move back to the house, only days after she'd insisted he move out and remove all his stuff from the garage?

"Get some rest. I'll stop by tomorrow morning. All I can say right now is that the preliminary bloodwork showed that you're dehydrated. It could be due to the altitude, if you're not used to the high elevation. The IV should take care of that. I'll get the rest of your test results either tonight or first thing tomorrow morning. If everything checks out, I'll do my best to discharge you by two o'clock tomorrow afternoon."

"Thank you, Doctor," she said, smiling through the tears. What was she going to do now?

Chapter Thirteen

Noah unlocked the door to his apartment. Excited, Rosie and Briggs rushed to the door and tried to lick Charlotte. The girl giggled and gently pushed them away.

"Briggs! Rosie! Off," Noah commanded them.

"Don't be mad at them. They just want to say hi to me." Charlotte wrapped her arms around their necks. "I missed you both so much. How come you didn't visit me yesterday?"

Abby hadn't told her she'd rescheduled their visit?

"Rosie is so big." Charlotte petted the excited dogs. "How long till the puppies come?"

"Sometime next week." He tousled Charlotte's hair.

"Can I hold them?"

"Not at first, but as soon as Rosie lets us, you can play with them as much as you want."

"Really?" She let go of the dogs and threw her arms around Noah's waist. "You're the best, Noah. I love puppies. They are the cutest things in the entire world."

Noah's heart melted a little more at that moment.

Just then, his phone chimed.

"Hello?"

"Hey, it's me." Abby's voice sounded muffled.

"Hey there! What did the doctor say? Are you okay?"

"Yes, but I… I need your help."

"Sure, what is it?"

"I need you to stay at the house for a few days. Would you be able to do that?"

Noah sat on the sofa and watched Charlotte play with Briggs while he focused on Abby's words. Had God just answered his prayers?

"No problem. How about I let you talk to Charlotte, so you can explain to her what's going on?"

He handed the phone over to the girl and watched her face light up as soon as she heard her mom's voice. Noah was walking toward his bedroom, making a mental list of what to pack, when Charlotte's excited scream startled him.

"Noah. Mom says you can stay at our house while she gets better." She jumped up and down, leaving Noah to wonder what Brenda, the ever-complaining super, would say if she ever got wind of this. "And Briggs and Rosie, too. I asked and she said yes!" Charlotte shoved the phone at him and spun around, obviously searching for something. "I need a bag," she said to Noah, completely ignoring that he was trying to talk to Abby.

"Hold on," he said into the phone. "Bag for what?"

"I need to pack the dog toys," she said in an exasperated tone. "And their food, of course."

Noah chuckled.

"Sorry, Abby. Someone here is a little bit excited." He looked at Charlotte. "Let me finish talking to your mom and then we can pack everything together. Okay?"

The girl dropped onto Rosie's dog bed and pursed her lips, her eyes not leaving him.

Noah laughed out loud.

"Abby, I'm sorry, but I really have to go, Charlotte is giving me the eye. How about I call you from the truck on the way up the mountain?"

He ended the call, shoved the phone into his back pocket and met Charlotte's gaze.

"Tell you what." Noah reached for a half-empty box on top

of the stack. He tipped it over and spilled the contents onto the sofa. "Let me pack some of my clothes and you can fill this with anything you think Briggs and Rosie will need."

"You got a deal." Charlotte sprang to her feet, grabbed the box and scurried to the kitchen. "Their food dishes first," he heard her say, her voice carrying through the small apartment. "Rosie really likes to eat."

Noah couldn't help but laugh some more. He went into the bedroom and filled his duffel bag with everything he'd need. Then he opened the bedroom closet, pulled out a vinyl craft case and reached to the upper shelf for a stack of construction paper.

"Ready?" The excited girl stood in the bedroom holding the overflowing box. "I've got everything."

He chuckled.

"What's that?" Her eyes zoomed in on the small yellow briefcase.

"I'll tell you as soon as we get to your house."

Charlotte squinted her eyes. "I see construction paper." She bit her bottom lip. "Do you like crafts?"

"As soon as we get to your house." He tapped her nose. "I promise."

"But I want to see what's in it," she whined.

"Rosie, Briggs." Noah clicked on the leashes. "Coming?" He glanced at Charlotte. Her bottom lip looked a little pouty.

Noah pushed the keys into the lock, balancing his bag, the craft kit and two eager Vizslas. "I've got to lock up."

"Okay," Charlotte said, dragging herself toward the door.

"Good." He smiled, shut the door and turned the key. "Thanks for all your help."

"No problem." Charlotte grinned up at him. "I'm a good packer."

"An excellent one." He held the front door of the building open for her. "You first, then me and the dogs. That way, no one gets tangled in the leashes."

Once everything was loaded and everyone buckled in, Noah started the truck. The dogs were excited, because a car ride usually meant a trip up the mountain.

As they passed the Hope Rock sign, Charlotte turned her head. "Are you and Mom friends?"

"I'd say so. What does she say?"

"She said you used to be friends a long time ago."

Noah tapped the steering wheel with his fingers, wondering what he should say about his and Abby's past.

"She cries a lot," Charlotte said in a small voice.

Noah stayed silent and kept his eyes on the road.

"I think she misses my dad."

"Uh-huh," he mumbled, silently praying God would give him the right words.

"I miss him, too." Charlotte looked out the window, then at Noah. "Will you forget me, too, if we're no longer friends?"

His heart splintered. He reached for her small hand.

"Charlotte…" He glanced at her. Their eyes met. Hers were filled with unshed tears. "I could never forget you."

She squeezed his fingers.

"Pinkie promise?" She let go of him and crooked her little finger.

"Pinkie promise," he said in a serious tone, his words heavy with the weight of the moment. He hooked his pinkie with hers. "Friends forever." He smiled, surprised at the thick lump that suddenly formed in his throat.

Charlotte was an extraordinary girl. He was very glad to help her and Abby out in their time of need.

Abby opened her eyes and stared up at the hospital room ceiling tiles. An IV was still taped to her arm and the monitors attached to her beeped in a steady rhythm. The fog had cleared from her brain, yet she still felt anxious. Charlotte was with Noah. Abby had no reservations about her former high school sweetheart. Despite all that had happened between them, Noah was one of the kindest people she had ever met. She frowned. So why, then, had he kissed Natalie? Had he thought Abby would never find out? But Noah wasn't a cheat. Was it her best friend who betrayed her and Noah simply went along? And what about his brother? Had Brad ever found out what had happened in the school parking lot?

She tried to turn to her side, but the lines attached to her made it impossible. Would she have to call a nurse every time she needed to move? Memories swirled through her mind. She had been so upset after the prom that she refused to talk to anyone, especially Noah. He had driven up to the cabin several times that summer, but Abby had instructed her parents to tell him she wasn't available. Why had she been so stubborn? Perhaps if she'd given him a chance, he would have explained what she had seen. Her eyes prickled with tears. The old heartbreak was still a painful memory. What could he have said? Especially after she saw him back at the gym, sitting with his brother and Natalie, her best friend, draped in Noah's tux jacket. They were laughing, sipping on punch, chatting like everything was normal—while Abby's heart had been shattered.

Her back ached. Abby reached for the call button and pressed it once. Hopefully, the nurses weren't too busy. She couldn't stay in the same position much longer. She turned her head and looked out the window. The sky was clear and crisp, a few white clouds moving slowly across the window frame. Would her life have turned out differently had she given Noah a chance back then?

The nurse walked in, glanced at the monitors, then smiled at Abby.

"How are you?"

"Getting pretty stiff. Could you please help me sit up?"

"Of course." The nurse reached for her pillow, then assisted Abby.

A slight wave of dizziness swept over her.

"Are you all right?"

"I just need a minute," Abby said, breathless.

"Take your time." The nurse straightened up and watched her closely.

Abby looked up and mustered a weak smile. "Thank you."

"You're welcome. If you need anything, just buzz me. And please, don't try to get out of bed without my assistance."

"Of course," Abby assured her, wondering if the nurse had just read her mind. If only she could read Noah's.

The nurse rushed out, leaving Abby alone with her thoughts. Was it at all possible that she had misjudged Noah all those years ago? He had been nothing but kind to her since she and her daughter had arrived in town only a few short days ago. And his attention to Charlotte was so wonderful, it made Abby emotional. Perhaps she should ask him what happened after Abby left the town. Had he and Natalie dated? And what about the rest of the Ross brothers? Her old church and school friends? Why had she been so eager to move on and forget Hope Rock, cutting her parents off every time they tried to share a bit of news from her hometown? If she was serious about their new start, she would have to let go of all that and reconnect with her former friends. This was a small town, and things would get awkward real fast if she tried to avoid running into anyone she had known all those years ago—especially the handsome and kind Noah Ross.

Chapter Fourteen

Scrambled eggs sounded like a great dinner option, Noah and Charlotte had agreed during their ride up the mountain.

"And after we do the dishes, will you show me what's in that yellow case?" she asked him.

"I see you don't forget anything," he chuckled, parking the truck.

"Never."

"Okay, it's a deal." He got out of the truck, walked around the hood and held her hand as she jumped onto the driveway. "Why don't we let Rosie and Briggs sniff around for a bit while we unpack everything? I have a couple of old dog beds in the coach house, so maybe you can help me bring them in. We can set them up in the hallway."

Her ponytail swung as she nodded with unbridled enthusiasm.

"Then you will show me?"

He shook his head, picked up the bags and brought them inside. Leaving everything in the hallway, Noah spun around and strode toward the coach house. He opened the garage doors and walked in.

The two dog beds were stashed in the corner, right next to the pile of his boxes. He would have to talk to Abby about that, too.

"I'm here." Charlotte sprinted into the garage. "Can I carry Rosie's?"

"Of course." He passed her the top one. "Are you going to be okay? It's kind of big."

"I got it," she said confidently and marched across the drive-way toward the house, two eager dogs right at her heels.

Noah ran his fingers through his hair.

Lord, I asked before, but I'm asking again. This little one has my heart, and so does her mom. Please help me set things right.

Charlotte scarfed down her dinner of scrambled eggs and toast almost as fast as the dogs. She practically ran to the kitchen sink with her empty plate, rinsed it and set it on the drying rack.

"I'm ready."

"For what?" Noah scraped his plate.

"For the yellow case!"

"All right, then." He got up and pushed his chair back. "Just let me wash my plate first."

She took it out of his hands. "I can do that while you get the case."

He suppressed a laugh. This girl knew what she wanted. "Okay."

While Charlotte hurriedly scrubbed the plate, Noah brought the yellow craft kit from the hallway and set it on the table.

Charlotte ran up to him. "Can I open it now?"

"You've been so patient," he said, then chuckled. "I don't see why not."

She popped the lid open.

"Wow!"

Charlotte reached inside the case and ran her fingers over the colorful bundle of pipe cleaners and the elastic-bound Popsicle sticks. She picked up a clear bag of tiny glittery pom-poms.

"I've never seen these before. Mom and I only bought the plain ones at the dollar store." She set the bag down and reached for the bag filled with stick-on stars tucked inside the kit right next to a pack of googly eyes. "These are *so pretty.*" She exhaled the words.

Noah's craft supplies collection visibly amazed her.

"I love glitter." She reached for a sparkly tube. "And you

have three colors. And the special wavy scissors. Can we make something?"

"We have to make a crown for Lisa."

"A crown?"

"Yes, a birthday crown. I make one for everyone's birthday in my Sunday school class."

"You do?" Her eyes grew wide. "Will you make me one when it's my birthday?"

"Absolutely." Noah reached for the construction paper pad. "I think her favorite color is pink."

"Same as mine!"

"Let me cut it out and then you can help me decorate it."

"With glitter?"

"For sure. The only thing is, we need to keep it under control. It's very hard to clean up glitter."

"I know," Charlotte said in a somber voice. "My dad never let me have glitter in the house."

How could he respond to that? Noah reached for the scissors and cut out the crown. "Okay, your turn to make it dazzle," he said.

"I can do that." Charlotte reached for the markers and drew a row of hearts. "Everyone loves hearts," she said as she colored them in. "Dark pink and light purple go well together."

Noah leaned back in his chair and watched the little artist at work, his heart brimming with joy.

"Noah." Charlotte looked up. "When we're finished with Lisa's crown, could we make a card for Mom to make her feel better?"

"That's a great idea." He tousled her hair. "How about I make us a hot chocolate while you work on that?"

She beamed at him. "Can I have it in my favorite mug?"

"Which one is that?"

"The heart one, of course. But not the old one. That's Mom's."

Noah opened the cupboard and took out the two once-matching mugs. He held his well-used one in his hand. Had Abby been using it?

The crown and the card finished, the hot chocolate mugs washed, the whining dogs in the hallway, and Charlotte tucked in bed, Noah settled on the sofa. It wasn't the most comfortable place to sleep, but sleeping in the master bedroom was out of the question. Even though he had slept there for the past five years, it was Abby's room now. And completely inappropriate for him to be in there.

Rosie and Briggs took turns complaining behind the hallway door. If he vacuumed before Abby came home from the hospital, would she get upset that he'd let them in the house?

The door to Charlotte's bedroom creaked open.

"I can't sleep." Her tired voice tugged at his heart.

"Would you like me to read you another story?" Unsure if that would do the trick, he got up and walked toward her.

"I want Rosie."

He frowned. What should he do? Of course he wanted to abide by Abby's wishes. But right now, the best thing to do was to let Rosie snuggle up with the distraught child.

Noah held Charlotte's gaze. "I've got an idea. How about a campout?"

"Outside?"

"Why would we sleep outside if we have a perfectly good tent right here?" he said.

"What? Where?" Her eyes grew wide.

Noah pointed both thumbs over his shoulders. "Right there."

"In the dining room? I don't see a tent."

"Bring me some blankets."

Charlotte's face lit up. The girl sprinted around the living room and gathered up all the throw blankets in one huge heap, barely able to carry them all.

"Now, allow me." A grin creased his face as he recalled the

countless forts he and Brad, his twin brother, had built during their childhood.

Charlotte stretched a blanket along the long side of the table.

"This is awesome." The excited girl clapped her hands.

"Let's look in the hallway closet for some sleeping bags."

Charlotte nodded and fluffed up the rest of the blankets, making sure the tent's walls were properly secured. Then she crawled in.

"Can I bring my flashlight? And my pillow?"

"Of course," he said, chuckling. Charlotte would probably sleep best with something familiar, he thought. "Why don't you go get them and I'll grab the sleeping bags." He opened the door. Two sets of expectant eyes followed him to the closet. Noah reached for the sleeping bags on the top shelf and went back into the dining room. The synchronized whining followed him, but the dogs stayed behind the closed door.

"Just give me a moment to set things up, you two," he whispered.

In the meantime, the excited child ran to her room and came back with two pillows, and her stuffed animal, and a pink flashlight stuffed in her pocket. Noah unzipped one of the sleeping bags and spread it under the table to soften the floor.

"Okay, camper Charlotte," he said with a smile, "throw in your pillows and settle in." He passed her the soft, rolled up sleeping bag. "Make sure you zip up, so no snakes crawl in with you."

Charlotte looked surprised, then caught on. "Okay, Counselor Noah," she said, her tone brimming with excitement. She crawled under and unrolled her sleeping bag. "Noah, where will you sleep?"

"The counselors' cabin is right over there." He pointed to the sofa.

"My tent has some unused bunks." Her timid voice tugged at his heart again. "There's room for a couple more campers here, if anyone needs a place to sleep."

Noah chuckled. This kid was too much.

"Well, we have a couple of late arrivals, so if you don't mind, I can assign camper Rosie and camper Briggs to your tent."

"I don't mind at all."

He heard the smile in her voice.

"They might be a little excited by the news, so you need to tell them to lie down and go to sleep. No talking after midnight."

"Okay," she whispered, with a tiny hint of disappointment in her tone.

Noah opened the hallway door and the two dogs rushed in. They sniffed around for a moment, then discovered Charlotte's *tent*. Both of them ran in, excited by the unusual development. Charlotte giggled as the dogs licked her face. Noah stood by the table, making sure the dogs didn't pull down the blankets.

"Okay, campers," he said in a soft voice. "Simmer down."

The soft rustle of the sleeping bag confirmed that the dogs were finding their preferred spots to lie down.

"Can I keep the flashlight on for a bit longer?" Charlotte whispered.

"Lights out in five minutes, and then all of you have to go to sleep. We need to get up pretty early, because I have a little surprise for you in the morning."

"A surprise?" Her voice was a little too excited for a child who needed to settle down. "I love surprises."

"Okay, but you'll have to be quiet now. Rosie needs her sleep. Her puppies will come in a few days and she'll be a busy mama. So, now is the time for her to rest up."

"Yes, Counselor."

Charlotte fluffed up her pillows. "Rosie, put your head here," she instructed the dog. A soft rustle followed. "Briggs, you can snuggle closer to me. Rosie needs a little bit more room for the puppies in her tummy."

Noah's throat thickened. Despite what Charlotte had endured recently, her sweet, innocent heart was filled with love and kindness, and he would do his utmost to help her keep it that way.

"Good night, Rosie," the little voice whispered. "I love you. Good night, Briggs." The sound of a kiss melted Noah's heart. "I love you, too."

He sank into the sofa cushions. This girl reminded him so much of what was missing from his life. He desperately wanted a family. A wife and kids. But it just hadn't happened for him. Yet.

But he hadn't given up hope. In fact, with Abby and Charlotte's arrival in Hope Rock, things were looking up in that regard.

"Good night, Noah."

"Good night, Charlotte," he called out as he turned off the side table lamp.

"I love you," the little voice said softly. Her flashlight clicked off.

"I love you, too," he replied into the darkness.

The constant beeping of the monitor kept her awake, and the random noises in the hallway disrupted her sleep. Abby turned to her side, took a deep breath, then exhaled. She was exhausted, but despite her need for rest, her mind kept whirling. How was Charlotte doing? Which bedroom had Noah chosen for himself? How would she manage if he was constantly there with them at the house? Wasn't Rosie due to have her puppies any day now? Did it mean there would be puppies running through her house? How would she be able to proceed with the house renovations with a pack of dogs there? She reached for her cell phone. Charlotte would be asleep, but she could try to text Noah.

Hey! she texted.

Abby touched the Send icon, her eyes not leaving the screen. A long-forgotten sensation bubbled up in her chest. The excitement caused by the anticipation of his reply surprised her. Her phone buzzed—an incoming text.

Feeling nineteen again, she glanced at the screen.

She's asleep. Everything went well.

An instant jab of disappointment deflated her. Of course, he would think she was messaging him about Charlotte. Why else would she? They weren't a couple. They hadn't been for years, despite his attempts to repair things between them a long time ago.

Her phone vibrated.

How are you feeling?

Abby smiled.

I'm fine.

Does the doctor know what caused you to faint?

She was unsure how much to tell him.

He's running more tests but said they might let me go tomorrow afternoon.

The dots on her screen indicated that Noah was typing. A strange exhilaration flooded her chest. Then the dots vanished. Then a new message popped up.

Charlotte will be thrilled. As I tucked her in, she kept asking me when you'd be home. She's a great kid, Abby.

Thanks!

Perhaps this was the time to ask him if he would be able to stay for a week or two until Dr. James dropped the social services threat. She typed her request, then quickly sent it before she could change her mind.

Noah had his dogs, his job and an apartment in town. Abby hated being this needy. But who else could she ask? And what if he said no? Hopefully, Abby could get her driver's license back before school started.

Sure, I can stay. We can sort out the details once you're home. I slept on the sofa tonight. I hope you don't mind.

She was surprised by his response, as if staying up at the cabin with her and Charlotte was the most natural thing in the world. But how many nights could he sleep on that old sofa before his back gave out?

Of course.

The dogs are staying in the hallway. Charlotte wanted them to sleep in her bed, but I didn't think that was what you wanted.

She felt a pang of guilt. Maybe she should have told Charlotte it was okay to snuggle with one of the dogs. She was practically in love with Rosie, and the dog would bring her much-needed comfort. Having Noah there, with the two dogs, was the best thing for Charlotte. But she worried that she'd get too attached to him and her little heart would break all over again once Noah left.

How long would you be able to stay?

As long as you need me to.

Abby gripped her phone a little tighter, recalling the promise she had made to herself, never to *need* a man again. Both of the men she had once loved and trusted had betrayed her. Breaking her heart was one thing, but hurting Charlotte? Never would she allow that.

We can talk about the details tomorrow once I know more, Abby typed fast. It was time to finish the text exchange.

I'll pray that all goes well and you can sleep in your own bed soon.

She'd had no idea Noah was the praying type. When did that happen?

Thank you.

Would you be okay with me taking Charlotte to church tomorrow morning? I could try to get someone to take over my Sunday school class, but it would be a super short notice.

Was Noah teaching Sunday school? He hadn't attended church when they'd dated. When had he started?

Sure.

One more thing. I have a puppy I'm taking care of at the clinic. I would need to bring it up the mountain, too. Would you be okay with that?

No problem. Thanks again.

After sending the message, she sank deeper into her pillow. She was so grateful to Noah for stepping up and taking care of Charlotte. What could she do for Noah to let him know how much she appreciated all that he had done for her and Charlotte?

Chapter Fifteen

As soon as her eyes opened, on Sunday morning, Abby prayed that the doctor would let her go home today. She couldn't spend another day here. Her thoughts had kept her awake until the early morning hours. Only after she'd been completely exhausted had Abby able to tune out the constant noise and fall asleep.

She would talk to Noah today. Their lives had taken them in different directions since prom night. But the fact that he stayed close to her parents for all these years, when she had chosen not to visit very often, still made her feel a little guilty. Back then, she had been too self-centered, unwilling to listen and forgive. But life had not turned out the way she had imagined. Perhaps she should give Noah a chance to explain what happened all those years ago.

Abby glanced at her phone. Was 7:00 a.m. too early to call? Noah said he was taking Charlotte to church, so perhaps they were already up. She opted to text him in case she was wrong.

Good morning.

Hey, good morning. How did you sleep? Noah's instant reply brought a smile to her face.

Terribly. Can't wait to be back in my own house. How about you?

You may need to get a new sofa if you're planning to have overnight guests.

She giggled and pressed the phone icon.

He picked up on the first ring.

"Hi," she said into the phone.

"Hey."

She could hear the smile in his voice.

"Why haven't you used the bed in the spare room? The cot should still be there."

He cleared his throat.

"Charlotte and the dogs camped out under the dining room table and I wanted to keep an eye on them."

"Under the table?"

"She was a bit anxious last night, so I let her pretend we were camping. The dogs loved it."

"I bet. Is she up yet?"

"Brushing her teeth."

"What time is church?"

"Sunday school starts at nine, so we're getting ready right now. I made her a grilled cheese sandwich, per her orders. We need to head out as soon as the dogs are done going outside and have food in their bowls."

A strange feeling washed over her suddenly. She was missing out on a perfect Sunday morning. Wasn't this what she had wished for all those years with her husband?

"When are they going to let you go home?" Noah's voice interrupted her thoughts.

"I don't know yet," she said, letting out a long sigh. "Noah, I've been thinking…"

"Yes?"

Abby mustered up her courage and went on. "I need to ask you a favor. It's pretty big, so if you can't or won't, please be honest and tell me. I don't want you to feel obligated to—"

"Abby, just tell me what you need."

"I need you to stay with us for a couple of weeks. The doctor won't release me from the hospital unless there's an adult staying with us, in case I get another dizzy spell. He's concerned about Charlotte's safety."

Without a moment's hesitation, he answered, "Count me in."

That took her by surprise. "Are you sure?"

"Absolutely."

"We'll have to talk about the logistics," she said, her voice cautious. "Rosie's due to give birth in a couple of days, right?"

"Abby, we'll make it work. How about Charlotte and I swing by the hospital right after church and we can talk this over?"

"That sounds great."

"Hate to cut this short." Noah's tone was apologetic. "But we really have to get going. The campers are ready for breakfast."

"Of course. Thank you. I'll see you after church."

She disconnected the call and held her phone close to her chest. This guy was something else. He was ready to step into the mess of her life and help her in her time of need. But was she prepared to let him? How would she deal with seeing him every day? Wearing those cowboy boots. Driving his red truck. Smiling at her from underneath his Stetson.

Just then, a nurse knocked at her door.

"Good morning. Breakfast will be here shortly. Dr. James will stop by afterward and talk to you about letting you go home later this afternoon."

"Thank you." This was the news she had been hoping for. Abby closed her eyes and imagined her kitchen, Noah and Charlotte standing side by side at the stove, flipping pancakes. She smiled. She could definitely get used to that.

When Noah walked into the Sunday school classroom, a swarm of ten excited kids ages six to eight surrounded him.

"Noah, look at this," Lisa shouted, showing him something.

"It was my birthday this week. My grandma got me my very own Bible. It's pink!"

"Great, and happy birthday to you, Lisa."

She nodded eagerly and smiled.

"Noah, Noah." Jamel waved at him. "My dad said I could play football this season if I keep my grades up."

"I'm sure you can do that." Noah took a step into the room. "I need you guys to take your seats, because we have a new person joining our class today, and I would like to introduce her to all of you."

The kids scrambled to the colorful beanbags arranged in a wide circle.

"All right, everyone." He smiled at his class. "This is Charlotte. She's new to town, so she doesn't know too many people yet. But I'm sure you'll all make her feel welcome."

"Hey, Charlotte." Max waved his hand.

Charlotte looked at the ground.

"Okay, why don't you find a seat, and once you feel a little more comfortable, you can tell us three things about you."

Charlotte nodded, then scanned the room, looking for a beanbag to sit on.

"Here." Anabelle patted a pink one next to her. "Sit here."

Charlotte smiled and walked toward the offered spot.

"Great. Why don't we open with some prayer and then talk about our week? If anyone has a prayer request, please tell us so that Chrissy can write it down. Are you okay with that?"

Chrissy nodded vigorously, got up and picked up a notepad and a pen off a side table.

"We'll leave the prayer sheet on my desk, so if anyone feels they would like to add to it during the class, they can do so. Who would like to start?"

Mark put up his hand.

"Go ahead, Mark."

"My prayer request is for my grandpa. He's supposed to come

and visit before the end of the summer, but his knee is hurting and he isn't sure if he'll be able to come."

"Thank you," Noah said and looked at the other children in the circle. A few other kids chimed in.

"Would you like us to pray for something?" Noah asked Charlotte.

"For my mom," Charlotte said quietly.

"What about?" Chrissy asked.

Charlotte looked up.

"So I can write it down," the girl added.

"She's in the hospital." Charlotte's voice cracked.

"Is she okay?" Anabelle asked.

"I hope so." Charlotte was clearly struggling to keep her tears at bay.

"She will be," Noah interjected. "Because when this class prays, God listens. Right, kids?"

Everyone nodded in agreement.

"If anyone thinks of anything else during the class, please feel free to add that to the list. Now, let's get to today's lesson."

Everyone settled down to listen.

"We'll be talking about forgiveness." Noah got comfortable on his beanbag. "Who in this room has had to forgive someone for something?"

All hands shot up.

"Anabelle, why don't you start?"

"My sister. She took my favorite sweater without permission, then wore it to art class and spilled paint on it."

Noah nodded, then called Jamel's name.

"My dad thought I was lying when I was telling the truth. Later, he said he was sorry, and I forgave him."

"Thank you for that example, Jamel, because owning up to our mistakes is a big deal. Why don't we talk about instances when you had to ask for forgiveness?"

Only one hand shot up.

"Chrissy, thank you for being brave enough to share."

"I said a mean word to a friend, and when I prayed before bed, I just couldn't get that out of my mind. So, the next day at school, I said I was sorry."

"And how did your friend react?"

"She said whatever, so I don't really know if she forgave me."

"What matters is that you owned up to your mistake and apologized to her."

Chrissy didn't seem convinced.

"Very good. Okay, let me tell you a story. There was this boy who loved his mountain bike. Let's call him Dave. One day, Dave went out for a ride with a group of his friends. He got into an argument with one of them. The other boy got very angry. When Dave wasn't looking, he took a sharp tool and poked holes in Dave's tires."

The class murmured with disapproval.

"Dave was very upset."

The kids nodded in agreement.

"He couldn't ride his bike. How would he get back home? He needed to figure out how to reinflate the wheels. Dave's dad had asked him to mow the lawn before he went out on the bike ride."

"And did he?" Charlotte asked.

"Nope. But now he needed his dad to come and help him fix the tire, but he was really scared to call him."

"I'd be scared, too," someone said.

"So, what were Dave's choices?"

"He could walk the bike home," Jamel called out.

"Or he could call his dad and tell him he was sorry for not mowing the lawn and tell him what the other boy had done," Anabelle added.

"I think you're getting there." Noah smiled. "But what about his friend?"

"I'd still be mad at him," Max said, joining the conversation.

"But Dave needed his dad to forgive him, too," Anabelle added. "I think he should forgive his friend."

"He needs to say sorry first." Jamel frowned.

"What if people don't?" Charlotte said, then looked to the floor.

"Sometimes it is difficult to forgive." Noah got up and walked toward her. "But we can always ask God to help us."

Charlotte nodded.

He smiled reassuringly. They would have to talk more later, since it was time for today's activity. "Anabelle, would you please pass around the sheets?" He gave her a stack of papers.

The kids got busy working on the puzzle. The classroom hummed with their chatter, and Noah thanked God for the opportunity to spend the morning with these sweet children.

He checked his watch—it was time for their little birthday tradition.

"Lisa."

Her eyes lit up.

"Would you please come here?"

The girl sprang to her feet and walked to Noah. Her excitement was palpable.

He opened one of the cupboards and took out the birthday crown that he and Charlotte had hidden there before the class.

"May I?"

Lisa nodded enthusiastically.

Noah placed the crown on Lisa's head.

"I love it!" The birthday girl beamed. "Pink is my favorite color." She adjusted the crown. "Thank you, Noah, it's beautiful."

"Actually, Charlotte did most of the work."

Lisa turned to Charlotte. "Thank you. I love sparkles."

"Me, too." Charlotte smiled.

"All right, class, let's sing…" Noah said.

The children started to sing "Happy Birthday" to their friend.

"And as tradition dictates," Noah announced, "this birthday girl gets not only a crown, but also a gift card to the Lickety Split ice cream parlor for a very special treat."

"Thank you!" Lisa said, accepting the envelope from him.

"You are most welcome. Happy birthday, Lisa. Before we finish, here is a quick reminder." Noah picked up the prayer request sheet. "Before we go, let me remind everyone that some of our prayers are only between us and God, and that all prayers are private, so we don't tell others about what we have prayed for—that's called gossip. I trust each one of you understands what I mean."

The class murmured in agreement.

"All right, I will need two volunteers to help me tidy up, and the rest of you can wait outside the classroom for your parents to pick you up." The room quickly emptied out. Anabelle and Charlotte stayed behind and arranged the beanbags in a neat row. Noah was glad that Charlotte had made a friend in the class. He glanced at the prayer sheet. A line was added at the bottom. It read, *For me and Mom to forgive Dad.*

Chapter Sixteen

Later that morning, Dr. James entered Abby's hospital room, wearing a pristine white coat, his stethoscope tucked in his front pocket. Abby held her breath as his warm brown eyes met hers with genuine concern.

"Good morning, Ms. Clifford." His deep voice carried authority. He picked up her chart and glanced over the notes.

"Morning, and please call me Abby." She wouldn't explain to him right at this moment that just the sound of her ex-husband's last name made her cringe. But it was also Charlotte's last name. That was the only reason she had opted to keep it instead of reverting to her maiden name.

He read over the nurse's notes. "I see your bloodwork is looking good now. How are you feeling?"

"Anxious to get out of here." Was that the right thing to say? If she wanted him to discharge her today, she probably shouldn't be telling him that she had stressed over the arrangements she had been forced to make. Asking for help from others was not a strength of hers.

"I see." He looked up and held her gaze. "Frankly, I don't see anything that would concern me right now. All the tests indicate that you are healthy. I would like to run another battery of tests a couple of days from now, but there's no reason for you not to go home right now."

Abby smiled. The conversation was going exactly the way she'd hoped.

The doctor tapped his pen on the clipboard.

"You just moved to this area, correct?"

"I was born here but lived in St. Louis for the past twelve years."

"Hmm," he said as he flipped through the papers. "Your hydration levels are normal now, but I would urge you to make sure you drink plenty of liquids for the next few days. Your body might need to acclimatize to the elevation."

Abby let out a pent-up breath, releasing her deepest worries. If dehydration was the cause of her blackout, she could definitely manage that.

"If you promise me that you have an adult staying with you for the next few weeks while we get to the bottom of this, I will discharge you today."

"Thank you, Doctor. I do have someone who'll be staying with me and my daughter, as you recommended."

The doctor nodded. "You'll need to come back and see me in my office on Wednesday. We'll run another blood test. I would like to keep an eye on things for a couple of weeks, just to make sure that you are doing well. And one more thing, Abby," he said as he slid her chart into the acrylic holder on the wall.

The doctor cleared his throat. "I might be overstepping here, but a divorce is nothing to be ashamed of. And you need to take care of yourself. I'm here to help—and there are others in this community who would gladly do the same. You don't have to go through this alone. All you need to do is ask for help."

Abby swiped at her tears. Charlotte needed her to be whole and healthy. She owed it to her daughter to be the best version of herself.

"I…it's hard for me," she said, her voice breaking.

He nodded. Stepping closer, he placed his hand over hers. "You will get through this."

Abby sniffled.

"I'll tell the nurse to prepare your discharge papers and set up an appointment with my office this week."

Abby nodded and reached for a tissue.

"Your discharge papers should be ready by two o'clock," he said and patted her hand. "You will be okay, Abby. I promise."

She tried to smile through her tears, unable to believe his words fully. The only thing that made her somewhat happy was that Charlotte would be here soon and she could hold her sweet girl again.

Dr. James left the room, and Abby leaned back against the pillow. She exhaled.

Abby looked at her phone. Church should be over by now. She typed out a text message.

The doctor promised to discharge me by two.

We'll pick you up right after lunch, Noah wrote back.

Thanks!

A smile crossed her face, imagining Charlotte munching on some special treat Noah had surely gotten for her. The two of them were getting along really well.

Maybe too well.

If Charlotte got too attached to him, how would she handle Noah moving out when the time came? Abby would have to think about that when she got home. She needed to explain to her daughter that Noah would be staying only temporarily.

Abby rested her head on the pillow for a moment and looked out the window. She was so tired of all of this. Of suppressing her feelings so Charlotte wouldn't see her upset, of being angry at Noah for something that happened over a decade ago, of being mad at God for letting her life fall apart like this.

It was time for a change.

* * *

"Mommy!" Charlotte let go of Noah's hand, and he smiled as he saw her run to Abby. This girl had such a pure heart that it made him choke up. She was sweet, resilient and not afraid to ask God for help when she needed it.

"Hey there." He stepped closer to the bed.

Abby sat up straighter. "I'm just waiting for the nurse to unhook me from all the monitors and we can get out of here."

"We made you a card, Mommy," Charlotte said, handing her the construction paper sheet, folded in half, covered with hearts and sparkles. "To help you feel better."

"Thank you, honey." Abby opened it and looked it over, a huge smile on her face.

Noah pulled up a chair. "Tell me what the doctor said." When she hesitated, he went on, "You don't have to, but it would help all of us to know what to expect."

"He isn't sure yet what's wrong. I need to see him on Wednesday for a follow-up." Abby took a deep breath. "Noah, I'll need you to stay with us for a couple of days, while this gets sorted out. Are you sure you can do that?"

"No worries," he responded. He would have to tread carefully. Abby needed time to rest and recuperate. "I was actually thinking—" He leaned forward. "Why don't I clear out the old loft apartment above the garage? It's not been in use since I moved to the house."

"You think it will be livable up there?" she asked.

"Sure, once we move the boxes out. I know of a great assistant." He winked at Charlotte.

"I can help, and so can Rosie and Briggs." Charlotte seemed to struggle to contain her excitement. "It will be like Noah has a cabin at our cabin," she giggled.

"And once we're done, we could set up the whelping box in the coach house garage."

"What's a yelping box?" Charlotte asked.

"The place for Rosie to have her puppies." Noah smiled catching her mispronunciation. He decided not to correct her. "They should be coming in the next few days."

"Yes!" Charlotte hopped off the bed and ran to Noah. She wrapped her arms around him. "I'm so excited for Rosie."

He looked over at Abby.

"And of course, I'll move the dogs to my place as soon as the doctor gives you the green light," he added.

"Why can't they stay in the garage?" Charlotte asked, her eyes darting between the adults.

"I think clearing out the loft is a good plan," Abby said. "We can deal with the puppies when the time comes."

Noah pressed his lips into a thin line. She needed him, but the coldness in her voice made him question his decision to move out of his condo and into the loft, even temporarily. He wasn't welcome at the cabin. That much was clear. How could he be on the property, knowing that she resented him and his dogs? His gaze rested on Charlotte. One thing was certain: This child needed him. There was no question in his mind that the doctor would call child services if he even suspected that there was no other adult at the cabin while Abby was recuperating. He silently promised Charlotte that he wouldn't let her down.

The nurse walked into the room.

"Hey." She smiled at Noah. "Fancy seeing you here, Dr. Noah. I'll have to tell Naya that she had missed out." The nurse chuckled.

"Mrs. Swanson." Noah smiled, recalling her cat's visit to the veterinary clinic. The feline had hurt one of her claws while climbing the curtains. "Naya knows where to find me," Noah replied in a playful tone. "Although her last visit was a bit dramatic."

"That's an understatement." The nurse walked toward the monitors. "I can still hear her yowling while you stitched up her paw." Then she looked at Abby. "I got your discharge papers. Just sign at the bottom." She passed her the papers. "And here is your appointment card to see Dr. James on Wednesday."

She pressed a few buttons, and the monitor screen shut off.

The nurse leaned closer to Abby. "Let me unhook you and you're free to go." She deftly detached all the wires.

"Thanks so much."

"Have a great day," she chimed. "See you around," she said, smiling at Noah as she left the room.

"We'll wait in the hallway while you change into your street clothes." Noah stretched his arm toward Charlotte. The girl gripped his fingers and followed him out.

As he shut the door behind them, the nurse retraced her steps down the hallway.

"Dr. Noah." She turned to face him. "I just want to thank you again for helping Naya. The kids were so worried."

"Who is Naya?" Charlotte interrupted.

"Our cat," the nurse replied.

"How is she?" Noah inquired.

"Doing much better. I can't thank you enough." The nurse touched his arm just as the door of Abby's room opened.

"Noah, could you—"

He turned toward the door. The instant pain in Abby's eyes caught him by surprise.

"Thanks again," the nurse said. "And I'll get a wheelchair for our patient." Her eyes rested on Abby.

"Never mind," Abby said, walking back into the room and picking up her bag. "I'm ready whenever you are."

"Let me help you," Noah offered to Abby, extending his free arm.

"I'm fine," she replied in a clipped tone. "And you can tell your friend that I don't need a wheelchair."

"Can I ride in it?" Charlotte chimed in.

"No," Abby snapped.

"Is everything okay?" Noah scowled, still holding Charlotte's hand.

"Of course, why wouldn't it be?" Abby quipped and held out her arm to her daughter.

Charlotte grabbed Abby's free hand, turned to Noah and grinned.

"Now you can swing me."

Unsure of what Abby's reaction would be, Noah hesitated.

"Come on," Charlotte said in a singsong voice and started down the hallway, pulling the adults along. "You have to walk a little faster, so I can pretend I'm a monkey." She swung her arms to the rhythm of their steps.

Noah glanced at Abby. Her face was a mask.

"A monkey?"

"Yeah, Mom knows the game. You have to count backward and then swing me." She giggled. "Right, Mom?"

"Not now, Charlotte."

"But Mom—"

"I said, *not now.* Let's go home."

Charlotte went quiet.

Noah wished he could break this icy mood.

"Ms. Clifford," the nurse's voice echoed through the hall. "I'm afraid I have to insist on your using the wheelchair. It's the hospital policy." Nurse Swanson pushed the empty chair toward them.

"Take a seat, please."

Abby hesitated for a moment but eventually settled on the plastic seat.

"Thank you," the nurse said politely and rushed off in the direction of the nurses' station.

"Can I push you?" Charlotte asked, unmistakable excitement in her voice.

"Sure," Noah replied, one hand on the back of the chair. "If that's okay with your mom."

Abby nodded. "Let's get out of here."

The hospital entrance door swished open, and as they passed through, Noah prayed that God would grant him the wisdom to wait, the patience to stay, and the strength to love them through the ache, as they walked this journey toward healing. For even with Abby's guarded heart, wary eyes, and occasional grumpy attitude, he could no longer picture a life without her laughter or Charlotte's light. That thought settled over him like a promise, fragile yet steady, as they stepped together into the bright Sunday afternoon.

Chapter Seventeen

"I'm sorry for snapping," Abby said as soon as she put on her seat belt in Noah's truck. "It's just that so much has happened over the past two days, and I don't know how I'll cope with all the changes." She looked at the man sitting beside her. His brown eyes fixed on hers. "How will I ever repay you for all this kindness, Noah?" she asked softly.

He moved as if about to reach for her hand.

"It's okay, Mommy," Charlotte's voice chimed from the back seat. "We know you weren't feeling well."

"Thanks, baby." Abby turned toward Charlotte.

Noah gripped the steering wheel. "I'm just glad you're okay. You gave everyone a pretty good scare." He glanced at her once more, then checked the traffic in all directions and pulled out of the hospital parking lot.

"Mommy, Noah and I were pretend camping last night, and I really like Sunday school. Noah and I made a birthday crown for Lisa. And I have a new friend, Anabelle." Charlotte's words were filled with so much excitement that Abby couldn't help but smile.

"And we prayed."

"Prayed? What about?"

"So you get better and I find a way to forgive."

"Forgive?" Abby turned in her seat so she could see her daughter's face.

"Forgive Dad," Charlotte said in a small voice.

A thousand little needles pricked at Abby's heart.

"And I think Jesus heard us." Charlotte's voice was filled with excitement. "You got better and I didn't feel as sad when I thought of Dad this morning."

"That's wonderful, honey." Abby smiled at her, then turned back in her seat. She had left her with Noah for less than two full days and suddenly her daughter was praying? Despite her reservations, Abby felt a glimmer of hope. Charlotte sounded so happy. And she had Noah to thank for that. Abby reached toward the driver's seat and laid her hand on Noah's arm.

"Thank you," Abby murmured.

He kept his eyes on the road, but a smile broke out on his face.

"Mommy."

Apparently, there was more news Abby needed to catch up on. "Yes, honey?"

"I'll be helping Noah to build a yelping box for Rosie today."

"Yelping box?"

Noah chuckled. "Whelping box," he corrected.

"The puppies are coming soon." Charlotte clapped her hands.

"About that." Abby turned toward Noah. "Would you like us to stop at your place? We can help you move some of your stuff back to the chalet."

"I don't think you're in any condition to carry boxes down two flights of stairs."

"Noah, there is nothing wrong with me. I promise you."

He clenched his jaw, and Abby wondered what he was trying not to say. After a moment, he switched on a signal and turned left.

"If you're really sure, then I'll take you up on the offer. Rosie will need a few things, and I'll need some clean scrubs for work tomorrow."

He parked in front of a brand-new building.

"You live here?" Abby asked.

"Yep."

"In an *apartment*." Charlotte pronounced the word carefully.

"Come on, Squirt," Noah said. He unbuckled his seat belt. "Coming?" He looked at Abby, and when their eyes met, she smiled.

They walked into the building and up the first flight of stairs. As luck would have it, Brenda the super was there sweeping.

"Good afternoon," Charlotte greeted her politely.

"Afternoon." The woman stopped and stared. "I'm glad to see those dogs gone," she said when Noah passed by her.

Noah remained silent as he pulled the keys to his condo out of his pocket, unlocked the door and let them all inside.

"Welcome."

Abby's eyes took in the stacks of unopened boxes scattered about the room.

"Oh." Abby bit her lip. Noah had no time to take care of his things, yet he'd agreed to help her out with Charlotte. He looked at her apologetically. "I haven't had a chance to unpack. One of our vets is away, and between work and the dogs—well, it's been a bit busy."

He obviously misunderstood her reaction.

"That's not what I—" Abby touched his arm. "You are evidently pressed for time, and I keep adding to your schedule."

"And I'm glad for that." His gentle smile wrapped around her like warmth, assuring her that Noah truly meant it.

"Noah, the lady on the stairs doesn't like Rosie and Briggs?" Charlotte asked him as she picked up a couple of chew toys from the floor.

"No, not really," Noah said.

"Well, *I* like them. I think they're the best dogs in the whole world."

Abby took a deep breath. This place was nice, and the large

windows let in plenty of light, but there wasn't enough space for two dogs as large as Rose and Briggs and a litter of puppies.

"Noah." She reached for his arm. "Why didn't you tell me?"

"Tell you what?" Their eyes met. And a wave of emotion washed over her.

"That there's a problem with the dogs staying here."

"There really isn't. I talked to my lawyer. There is nothing—"

"Noah, they are welcome to stay at the cabin as long as you need them to. They need to run, and Rosie will need more space when the puppies come."

"Yes!" Charlotte was jumping up and down with excitement. She dropped one of the chew toys. "I need a bag or a box," she said, picking it up. "And we have to make sure we remember to pack the puppy collars."

"Thank you," Noah said quietly, looking straight into Abby's eyes. "I really appreciate that."

"We better get going, because we have a bunch of work to do," she said, her tone playful. "That loft looks worse than this. And if Noah and the dogs are going to sleep there tonight, we need to move all the old stuff out and clean the place up. What do you say?"

"Are you sure you are feeling up to it?" He caught her gaze.

"Absolutely." She smiled at him. "I think that you staying up the mountain is a great idea, right, Charlotte?"

Charlotte's face beamed as she nodded her head, the ponytail bouncing. Abby could no longer deny the feelings in her heart every time Noah looked at her.

Noah picked up one of the empty boxes in the corner of the room.

"Charlotte, I have a few things ready for the puppies. They're on the kitchen counter. Could you pack them for me and tape the box closed?"

The excited child grabbed the cardboard out of his hand and rushed off.

"What would you like me to help you with?" Abby asked.

Noah hesitated. He couldn't ask her to pack his clothes. But he hesitated to give her anything strenuous to do. "Do you think you can handle taking the dog blankets down to the truck?"

"Sure." Abby picked up the pink one and tucked it under her arm. "Pass me the other one, please."

Noah lifted it off the floor, and as he tried to hand it to her, their hands touched. He glanced up, and when their eyes met, he felt a rush of emotions. She blinked, then looked down at the floor, and Noah wondered if she felt the same. He cleared his throat. The more time he spent with these two…

"The puppy box is ready, Noah." Charlotte tugged at his sleeve.

"Great. Why don't I grab some of my clothes and then we can head back to the cabin? If I think of anything else I've left behind, I can always stop by after work and pick it up."

The little procession of the impromptu moving party descended the stairs. Brenda was still standing there, eyeing them.

"Goodbye," Noah said as he passed her.

"'Bye, Dr. Ross," Brenda replied.

Charlotte looked around the hallways. "Who is Dr. Ross?"

"That would be me," Noah chuckled.

"I thought you were a technician. You're a veterinarian?" Abby shot him a look.

"Yes, ma'am." Noah held the door open for them. "Someone has to do it." Noah's chest tightened at her assumption, a dull ache stirring up in his chest. Had she not believed in him back then? Had that been a reason she left? Noah wanted to tell her that he had been capable then, as much as he was now—but instead he swallowed the sting. He excused her doubt, telling himself it came from the past they never quite mended.

Chapter Eighteen

Standing at the door to the cabin loft, Abby was thankful to Noah for convincing Charlotte that the dogs were not the best of helpers when it came to carrying boxes down the stairs. They had set up the dog blankets in the house garage and left Rosie and Briggs there for now, but only after Charlotte filled a huge mixing bowl with water—in case they got thirsty.

She took a deep breath. The air was heavy with the smell of dust, old cardboard and buried memories. Her eyes scanned the neatly stacked boxes sitting against the back wall. Was she ready for this? Charlotte skipped around, ready to help her dust and vacuum so Noah and the dogs could stay here. But Abby was unsure what the old memories would do to her. Noah used to live in this loft after she left Hope Rock, helping her parents around the property. And after the car accident, it was Noah who'd offered to pack up some of their belongings and store them here while he rented the log cabin from her. Yet he had left so many things that reminded her of them and her former life in the cabin. Had he hoped that she would one day come back, not only to go through the boxes but perhaps to stay? But that day had never come—until now.

Would opening all the old boxes trigger an avalanche of memories? And if another wave of grief took over, how would she keep from falling apart again?

"We've got our work cut out for us." Noah's voice interrupted her thoughts. "But if you don't feel up to it, we don't need to do it today."

He was so in tune with her emotions, it still surprised her.

"I'm good. Let's get it done."

"I brought a duster." Charlotte pulled a small duster out of her back pocket. "Where should I start?"

"How about we start taking the boxes out of the loft, down the stairs and then load them on the truck so that Noah can drive them to the garage at the house. It will be much faster than carrying them one by one over to the house. I will go through them later."

"Yes, Mommy." Charlotte dropped the duster and picked up the box on the top of the pile. "What's in this one?" she asked.

"Probably some of your grandparents' stuff," Noah replied.

"Can we look at it?"

"Not today," Abby said quickly. She caught Noah's concerned glance.

"We've got to get this place cleaned up, Squirt, and if we start looking through each box, we'll get nothing done."

"Can we look tomorrow?"

"Maybe," Abby said, then picked up two closed boxes.

"Here, pass them to me," Noah said. "I'll take them downstairs."

"I can't wait to see all the treasures inside. It's like a mountain of Christmas gifts but not wrapped in pretty paper."

Abby let out a long sigh. Although Charlotte thought sorting through the old stuff would be fun, it held no appeal for her.

She reached for another box. This one was marked with her handwriting.

Top Secret! DO NOT OPEN

She recognized the box filled with her teenage high school memories. There was no way she could let Noah see this. She set it down and gently pushed it into the corner, hoping that he was still downstairs and wouldn't see.

"Mom, pass me another one," Charlotte's excited voice chimed behind her.

"Here you go, sweetie," she said, handing her a small box labeled in Noah's handwriting.

Nightstand

Had Noah gone through all of her parents' things? But who else was there to move the items out of the drawers? She'd come back to Hope Rock right after the accident—but she'd only been here for two days. She'd attended her parents' funeral, then let Ken whisk her away back to St. Louis, to the sheltered life he had constructed—until he'd left.

"Mommy." Charlotte tugged at her sleeve. "Why are you sad? You don't want to move the boxes downstairs?"

Abby forced a smile. "I just thought of something, and it made me sad. But we have a job to do, so Noah can stay and doesn't have to drive back and forth to his apartment."

"What did you think about?" Charlotte's eyes held her gaze.

"It doesn't matter anymore." Abby swiped at the tears and smiled. "We have a project to finish, don't we?"

Charlotte wrapped her arms around Abby's waist.

"Yes, we do, Mommy."

"Could I have more boxes, please?" Noah asked as he came over to them. "Or is my crew ready for a break?" he teased.

"I got one for you." Charlotte picked up another cardboard box from the pile. "And I'm not tired, not one bit."

"Neither am I." Abby smiled smd playfully shoved a box at him. "It's time to sweep out the cobwebs and do some proper dusting around here, Dr. Noah. We can't have you living among all the dust bunnies, right, honey?"

"Yep, Rosie and Briggs don't like spiders."

"They don't?" Abby glanced at her as she loaded the third box into Noah's arms.

"Nope. I know, because I don't like spiders, either."

Noah chuckled and took the boxes downstairs.

Abby swiped at her brow. The fatigue was finally setting in, but she was determined to continue, eager to let go of the past and make space for the promise of a bright future—which would hopefully include one handsome vet and his two dogs. She smiled to herself and picked up another box, ready to pass it to Noah as soon as he appeared at the top of the stairs.

One look in Abby's direction and Noah knew that this wasn't the right time for this job. After her hospital stay, her emotions had to be all over the place. But if he needed to move in right away, they couldn't wait. He'd been able to get Dr. Gina to cover part of his shift tomorrow, but he would still have to go to the clinic in the afternoon. Would Abby let Charlotte come with him? He needed to talk to her about the puppy as well, but clearing this room and settling the dogs in for the night was a priority right now.

Noah's eyes rested on the girl. Charlotte was so perceptive, so in tune with other people's feelings, especially her mom's. But what was going on in the child's heart? People said that children were resilient, but could it be that kids kept their feelings inside and couldn't verbalize what was actually going on in their heads? Or perhaps adults were too busy with their own problems and didn't take time to listen? Noah would need to find a few minutes and bring this to Abby. But that would have to wait. Asking him to move in temporarily was already a big deal for her.

"Here you go." Charlotte passed him another box.

"Thank you." Just seeing the enthusiasm on her face warmed his heart. Noah rushed down the stairs and set the box against the back wall. If they stacked them properly, there would be enough space for the whelping box and Rosie's kennel, in case she needed a break from the puppies. He could even keep the rescue puppy here for a couple of days until his brother had time to drive down and pick it up. Noah was pretty grateful that Brad agreed to drive for five hours each way to get the little pup. All Noah needed to do now was plug in the space heater for the night.

There was no need to move everything into Abby's garage right away. Hopefully, she would find the time and strength to sort through the boxes over the next couple of weeks so they could donate what she no longer wanted to keep. He could help her with that.

Just then, a sweet voice called down the stairs.

"Noah, I have two boxes here, ready for you. But Mom says we should take a break."

Noah frowned. Was Abby okay? They had been at this for less than an hour and had moved only a small portion of the stuff downstairs. If she needed to stop, that would be fine. He could dust and vacuum around the boxes and finish moving the rest of them during the week. The dog beds would fit, and he hadn't brought too many of his things. He walked up the stairs, searching for more items to move to the garage.

The kitchenette was still barricaded with cardboard boxes containing her parents' belongings. Noah reached for the one closest to him. They needed to wrap this up. "Are we done for the day?" He caught Abby's gaze. She looked exhausted.

"I think so. Would you mind if we finished this tomorrow?"

"Of course. I can do a quick cleanup and set up the dog beds. We should be okay for the night."

"Thank you," Abby said and walked toward him, a box in her hands. "You have been amazing."

He caught the glimmer of hope in her eyes. Perhaps the Abby he had once adored was returning. He reached for the box in her hands.

"Here, let me help you." Their fingers touched, and Noah struggled not to drop everything to the ground right then and wrap her in his arms.

"I got it." Her attempt at a smile didn't fool him. Abby wasn't ready, and besides, a pair of little eyes was surely paying careful attention.

He cleared his throat. "Okay, I'll grab a couple more boxes on my way down and we can figure out what's for dinner. What do you say, Squirt?"

"I'm afraid all we might find in the cupboards will be mac and cheese." Abby sounded tired.

"I know how to make that." Charlotte chimed in. "If you help me boil the water." She reached for Noah's hand.

He noticed a cloud of worry pass across Abby's face.

"Why don't we get your mom to help out as well?"

"Yes, we can all cook together," Charlotte said in a singsong voice, heading for the stairs.

Noah looked at Abby. A silent question hung between them.

"Sure," she said and tucked the box under her arm. "Why not. Let's cook together."

Noah grabbed a few boxes off the counter and followed her down the stairs.

Chapter Nineteen

As they walked back toward the house, Abby had to hoist the box up a couple of times. It grew heavy in her arms, but she wouldn't ask Noah for help, she couldn't risk him asking questions about its contents.

As soon as they took off their shoes, Abby beelined toward her bedroom and put the box on the bed. She'd have to ask him to set some time aside tonight. Her anticipation of the long-overdue chat with Noah grew. Would she find the courage to open her heart to him? What seemed almost impossible for her came so naturally to Charlotte. Her daughter was pretty much smitten with Noah. Abby smiled to herself. The feeling was definitely mutual. What was that cute little nickname he had for her? Squirt?

She glanced in the dresser mirror and winced. She needed to clean up, so she took a few minutes to wash her face, run a brush though her hair and put on some lip gloss. Now she was ready to tackle dinner.

Charlotte and Noah were already in the kitchen, filling a pot. Abby took in the scene unfolding in front of her. Had she not always wished for this? Why couldn't her ex-husband have spent time with their daughter, even before things got bad between them? He'd always been too busy. Business came first. And if Abby dared to bring it up, he would scold her, then tell her she needed to be more grateful. Abby tried to put that bitter memory behind her and focus on the present. She was back home in Hope Rock, and all would be well.

"Mommy, come help." Charlotte's voice brought her back to reality.

"How about I set the table?" Abby walked into the kitchen, then reached into the cupboard. "You and Noah seem to have everything under control."

"Can we use the pretty dishes?"

"Sure." Abby chuckled. Using her mom's nice china for macaroni and cheese? Why not?

"And don't forget the ketchup," Charlotte reminded her. "I really like ketchup. Lots and lots of it." Her daughter looked at Noah in such an adoring way that it squeezed Abby's heart. Seemed there wasn't much she could do to stop this bonding from happening. But what if Noah got tired of playing dad and walked away from them? He had betrayed her once before. How could she be sure he wouldn't do that again?

Abby set the dishes on the placemats that were on the table. Maybe once Charlotte was at school, her days would be filled with homework and after-school activities. And she'd be too busy to hang out with the veterinarian.

"Mom." Charlotte put on her best angelic face. "Could I pleeease let Rosie and Briggs inside the house? They are really good, I promise. I will tell them to lie down under the table and not beg for food."

It had been a long day, and Abby was too tired to argue. "All right. But you know the rules. As soon as they start whining for food—"

"Thank you, Mommy!" Charlotte sprinted down the hallway to let the dogs inside.

"Well, that was delicious." Noah pushed away from the table. "I'd even say this was the best macaroni and cheese I've ever had. Thank you, Chef Charlotte, you are very good at this." He reached out and gently tugged at her ponytail.

"I know." Charlotte beamed.

Noah chuckled and glanced at Abby. "We've had a busy day," he said, holding her gaze. "Let's tidy up."

"I can take care of that," Abby replied.

"Are you sure?"

"I've got Charlotte to help." Abby glanced at her daughter, licking the last bits of ketchup off her lips. The two dogs stared at her with googly eyes, most likely stunned that the plate wasn't given to them to clean up.

"I see that." Noah chuckled. "So," he said as he picked up his plate and carried it to the kitchen, "if it's okay with you, I'll borrow the vacuum cleaner and get my place ready for tonight."

"Great," Abby replied.

Charlotte hopped toward the kitchen, the plate in her hands.

Noah continued. "I'll feed the dogs in the garage and leave them there while I finish up in the loft. I'll be back in about an hour to drop the vacuum off and chat about tomorrow," he said, walking toward the hallway closet, his two companions at his heels.

Noah took the vacuum cleaner out of the closet, wondering if moving back up the mountain had been a good idea. Perhaps he wasn't the best person to help her out, at least until they cleared the air between them.

Slipping out into the cold evening, he carried his cleaning tools toward the detached garage. The vacuuming didn't take long. While putting the fresh sheets over his old single bed, he thought about when he had lived at this property. He had gotten along really well with Abby's parents, always helping Mr. Burns around the property when needed. Her parents had always been loving and kind to him, and Noah had often wondered why Abby hadn't visited more often. Had that been because of him? Her husband? Had she argued with her parents?

As much as he tried to talk to her and find out, she'd completely shut him out of her life. Noah knew that her parents thought she had rushed into marrying Ken. It had broke his heart, because he'd secretly hoped that she would return to Hope Rock after her college graduation. But she'd returned only once, for her parents' funeral. Noah picked up an old picture frame that lay facedown on top of the dusty dresser. It was Abby and him, the night of the prom. Brad took it, as Natalie made them smile with her funny grimaces. Noah chuckled as her recalled the last time he felt complete. Abby's parents stood next to them, beaming with pride. She wore a floor-length pink dress, matching the pink corsage he'd given her. Abby looked so beautiful, she still took his breath away. Little did he know that after that night, none of their lives would ever be the same. Noah had to talk to her and finally find out what had driven them apart.

Chapter Twenty

"Hey," Noah said, surveying the space. "Is Charlotte asleep already?"

Abby was sitting on the living room sofa as he walked in, vacuum cleaner in hand. She closed her high school yearbook and quickly shoved it into the cardboard box, then pushed everything under the side table, hoping that he wouldn't notice.

"Yeah, she was pretty tired."

"I was impressed how much work she did. For a little thing, she sure carried a lot of boxes."

"Do you have a couple of minutes?" Abby asked. "I'd like to talk to you about Charlotte." She motioned toward the chair opposite the sofa, but Noah surprised her when he sat next to her. She reached for a throw pillow and hugged it against her chest. How could she start this unpleasant conversation?

"Noah—" She inhaled deeply. "First, let me say how much I appreciate everything that you've done for Charlotte—" She paused. "For us," Abby added quietly. She glanced up at him.

Noah caught her gaze and smiled. "You don't need to thank me."

"Yes, I do. You're going out of your way to help us. I just don't know what you expect in return."

"In return?"

Abby looked at the old, worn carpet. "I can't pay you." Her words caught. This was probably the wrong thing to say.

"Pay me? Why would you even think that?"

"I don't want you to feel that I'm taking advantage of you."

"Is that what you're worried about? I just want you to know that being here with the two of you is no inconvenience at all. And thank you for letting me bring the dogs up here. So, this is a mutually beneficial arrangement." He grinned.

"Okay, good." She smiled back at him. "There are a couple more things I would like to chat about."

"Sure." He leaned back, getting comfortable.

"Charlotte is very impressionable. She doesn't show it, but she has been through a lot since the divorce. I don't want her getting too attached to you and then—"

"Abby," Noah interrupted. "I really like your daughter, but if you're in any way uncomfortable or feel that I'm overstepping, just tell me."

"You're great with her. Ken—" Abby swallowed. "He was never like this with Charlotte."

"Like what?"

"You like doing things with her. Talking to her, teaching her about the dogs—" Abby's eyes watered. "You really care about my daughter, don't you?"

"Of course I do." He locked his eyes with hers. The feelings that she was experiencing were so unexpected, Abby didn't know what to say.

"I care about you, too, Abby." He reached for her hand.

This was Noah, whom she had fallen in love with all those years ago. The guy her teenage heart had thought she would spend the rest of her life with. He was The One, until—

"I—" He swallowed and moved a little closer. "I want to ask you something."

"Yes?"

"What happened...after the prom?"

Abby tried to pull her hand back, but Noah gently tightened his hold on her fingers.

"Please, you have to tell me. I've been wondering...struggling to understand for over twelve years, Abby."

Was this the right time to dredge things up? She'd thought they were making progress, perhaps even moving past that terrible night. Now this?

"Abby?" He whispered her name.

Her mind swirled with the memories of their love, the pain of betrayal and the years of wondering and agonizing if every decision she had made since that night had been a wrong one.

"I saw you…in the parking lot, kissing Natalie." She willed herself not to start crying.

"What? Wait a minute," he said. "What do you mean, you saw me kissing Natalie?" Noah looked directly into her eyes. "I've never kissed another girl."

Abby froze. A sick feeling filled her stomach. Had she been mistaken all those years ago?

"But your tux—"

Noah exhaled. "Someone spilled a drink on Brad and Natalie wanted to go get some fresh air, so I gave him my jacket."

Her eyes grew wide, then flooded with tears.

"When I saw you, sitting at the table at the gym, your jacket over Natalie's shoulders, I thought—" Abby gulped for air. This was too much. The truth descended on her like a heavy, dark blanket. She'd made a mistake. She had believed he'd betrayed her for all these years, when it was she who had shattered their love. Abby felt dizzy.

"I—" she stammered, then stood up. "I broke your heart, Noah. I'm so sorry."

He stood next to her. His arms were instantly around her waist.

Tears streamed down her cheeks, and he pulled her in close. She didn't push him away.

"Abby, I always loved you."

The dam finally broke, and Abby melted into his embrace. He held her against him.

"I know, and I've forgiven you a thousand times."

"How could you?" she asked through her tears.

He brushed a strand of hair from her wet cheeks. "I knew you would be back one day." He swallowed hard. "And I decided to wait."

"Is that why you stayed in town all these years?"

She lifted her face toward his, and he ran his finger over her cheeks, wiping her tears away.

He reached for her hand and gently kissed her fingers. "Yes," Noah whispered. "Abby, there had never been anyone else for me but you."

She blinked, and when he leaned closer, she was ready to accept his forgiveness—and perhaps even to forgive herself. Her arms tightened around his shoulders, and Abby took in a shuddering breath.

"Mommy." The door to Charlotte's room creaked open. "Did Noah bring back the vacuum yet?"

She quickly let go of him. Noah took a step back, then sat in the chair next to the sofa.

Abby cleared her throat.

"Yes, he did. Why don't you go back to bed? We have a long day ahead of us tomorrow."

"But I'm thirsty."

"Go back in, I'll bring you a glass of water."

The patter of her feet, followed by the rustle of the blanket, indicated she was back in her bed. Abby looked at Noah. She suppressed a chuckle. Reaching for the tissue box on the living room table, she wiped her nose.

"Why don't you let me bring her the water, so she doesn't pepper you with a million questions?" Noah offered.

"Thank you." She sank into the sofa and pulled another tissue from the box, grateful to have a moment to recover from what had just happened.

Now that they had cleared the air, where did that leave them? Abby wasn't sure.

* * *

When Noah finally extricated himself from Charlotte's room, he found Abby dozing on the sofa. Her beautiful face was soft in the glow of the floor lamp. She shifted slightly. What would Abby think if her eyes suddenly fluttered open and she saw him, standing there, staring at her?

Before he could talk himself out of it, Noah bent down and scooped her into his arms.

Making his way slowly through the hallway to the main bedroom, Noah stepped over the threshold and took the last five steps toward the bed. He set her down gently atop the comforter and reached for the throw blanket draped over the foot of the bed. He was careful not to wake her. There would be plenty of time to finish their conversation in the morning.

He stood there for a moment, thinking of the future all three of them could share. But before he let his imagination run wild, he and Abby would have to sort things out. Noah walked to the door and gently closed it behind him.

Back in the living room, he fluffed up the throw pillows. He would stay here tonight, just in case Charlotte woke up and needed something. Rosie and Briggs would be okay in the garage—it was still warm enough. If all went well tomorrow, he would finish the cleanup in the loft, move the rest of the important stuff over and build the whelping box. Rosie had only a few days left, and Noah was thankful that this transition was happening now, not when she had a new litter of puppies.

Noah reached for the lamp switch. Darkness flooded the room, and he tucked the blanket a little tighter around his shoulders. He whispered a prayer of thanks. The thought that God would give him a second chance with this amazing woman was more than he could handle. And Charlotte? That girl was simply wonderful. He'd be one blessed man if God saw fit to make Charlotte his daughter.

Lord, please, don't let me mess this up.

Chapter Twenty-One

The gentle rays of mountain sunrise filtered through the old curtains into her bedroom. Abby woke up. She looked around, slightly confused. The last thing she remembered was Noah offering to tuck Charlotte back in bed. Abby pushed up on her elbows. How did she get here? Had she slept in her clothes? Where was Noah? She pulled back her blanket and got up.

Abby ran her fingers through the mess of her hair. Her phone was on the nightstand, plugged into the charger.

Thank you, Noah.

She picked it up and glanced at the screen. It was nine thirty-seven. Abby couldn't remember the last time she had slept in like this. She better check what the two of them were up to. Abby opened the closet and reached for the first hanger. Pink was a good color for a day like this. She smiled, recalling last night's conversation. Her heart felt light, and she smiled at her reflection in the dresser mirror. There was a real possibility that her dream of a new beginning with Noah could still become a reality. The smell of fresh coffee greeted her as soon as she stepped into the hallway. Abby smiled again. She could get used to this. A quick peek into Charlotte's bedroom—the small bed was made. And there were no clothes on the floor or hanging over the furniture.

"Charlotte?"

"Mommy!" Her daughter ran down the hallway. "Noah and I were super quiet so you could sleep late. Did we wake you?"

"Of course not. What time is it?" She made her way into the kitchen.

"Good afternoon," Noah teased, an apron around his waist and a spatula in his hand. "How would you like your eggs?"

"Over easy," Charlotte chimed in. "Mom's favorite."

"I know," Noah said with a soft smile on his face as he passed her a cup of steaming coffee. "Just wanted to check if it had changed. Why don't you two grab a seat? Charlotte, here's your plate."

"Thank you." The excited child bounced toward the table. "Noah said that after breakfast, we can set up the yelping box for Rosie."

"If that's okay with you." He passed Abby a plate with toast, then turned to the stove and cracked four eggs into the pan.

"Of course." Abby joined her daughter at the kitchen table. "Do you need any help?" she asked him, looking his way over the rim of her Valentine's Day coffee mug.

"I can manage."

After he easily scooped the eggs onto two plates, he crossed the distance with them and sat at the table. "Who would like to say grace?"

"I will," Charlotte chirped. She clasped her hands together, squeezed her eyes shut and took a deep breath.

"Dear God, thank You for the good sleep we had and the good food we're about to eat. Thank You that Noah and Mom like each other again, and lets him stay with us, and that Rosie and Briggs liked the garage. And also, I pray that the puppies will come soon. Amen."

Abby looked at Noah. His eyes were on her. Had they almost kissed last night? She felt herself blush.

"Well, let's eat." Noah picked up his fork and cut into the eggs.

"Thank you for cooking breakfast." Abby buttered her toast. "But we need to talk about how we want this to work in the future."

Noah looked up from his plate.

"You can't keep sleeping on the sofa."

Noah nodded as he picked up a piece of toast and took a bite.

"I mean, we should be able to finish moving the rest of the boxes into the garage, so I can eventually go through them and sort everything. And we can help you clean."

"And don't forget—" Charlotte raised her index finger "—we have to build that yelping box for Rosie."

"Whelping," Noah corrected, chuckling. "It is called a whelping box, Squirt."

Abby set her fork down. Did Noah's nickname for her daughter seem a little too familiar? He was here to help out for now, but was he here to stay? Did she want him to?

"Abby—" Noah's voice cut into her thoughts. "I've got another favor to ask."

"Yes?"

"Can I bring the rescue puppy from the clinic today and keep him in the coach house? He needs to be moved, but with Rosie expecting her puppies any day now, I'm not able to introduce another dog right now. I need to keep them separated till Brad comes up, sometime over the next few days and takes him to his no-kill shelter in River Run."

"Brad?" Abby lowered the fork. The eggs suddenly tasted like sawdust. Did she dare to ask about Natalie, Brad's high school girlfriend and her former best friend?

"Yes. It would be in a kennel and it would come with a heating lamp, both on loan from the clinic."

"Sure." Abby twirled the fork. "And how is Brad?"

A smile broke on Noah's face. "He's doing great. Loves his job. They bought a house last year and are expecting their second child."

They? Brad was married and had a kid? Abby took a bite of her toast. And he was happy. At least his life turned out for the best, while poor Noah had lived alone in this old cabin. Abby fought the rising tide of guilt in her chest.

"Good for him," Abby mumbled. "What's his wife's name?"

Noah looked a bit surprised. "What do you mean? Natalie, of course."

Abby dropped her fork. "How did I not know that?"

"I thought you knew."

"How? You hadn't mentioned it."

"They've been married for five years. It's not like it's a secret."

"Who is Natalie?" Charlotte asked.

"An old friend of ours," Noah replied.

Abby pushed her chair back and got up. Then she sighed deeply. This was too much. Her former best friend was happily married, expecting a second child, while she was struggling to recover from a messy divorce and was asking the most wonderful man—whom she had dumped years ago without as much as an explanation—for favors. Hot tears flooded her eyes.

"Abby." Noah gently gripped her arm. "You have got to let it go."

She yanked her arm out of his grasp.

Charlotte's eyes grew wide.

"Are you fighting?" She looked from Abby to Noah.

"Sorry, honey," Abby said in a soothing voice. "We aren't fighting." Turning to Noah, she murmured, "Thank you for the breakfast," then she walked over and turned the water on and plugged the sink. She added a squirt of detergent.

As the water rushed in and bubbles filled the sink, Abby's eyes blurred. There would be no happily-ever-after for her, despite the feelings that were slowly coming to life like flowers in the dry garden after a spring rain. While she could imagine letting Noah back into her life, how would she face her former friends? Even if she begged them for forgiveness, she couldn't envision spending every family holiday sitting across the dinner table, thinking about the mistakes she had made. Abby picked up the scrubby and washed her plate.

Charlotte skipped toward the kitchen, her dishes and utensils in hand.

"Mommy, can I go with Noah to take Rosie and Briggs for a run?"

"Why don't you grab a dish towel and help me?"

Charlotte let out a short huff. "But the dogs miss me."

"Why don't I help with the dishes so they get done faster?" Noah said, setting his plate on the counter.

"You cooked, we clean. It's only fair," Abby said as she dunked his plate into the suds.

"But I helped Noah, so it's even more fair if he helps me." Charlotte picked up a fresh dish towel from the drawer and passed it to Noah. "And then I can help him with the dogs, right, Mommy? That's what friends do. And Noah is my friend. Yours, too. Right?" Charlotte skipped, a wet plate in her hand.

A friend.

Why did that word rattle in Abby's ears? Was Noah her friend? He was so different from the mom group besties and the business acquaintances Ken had introduced her to back in St. Louis. No one else had ever done anything like this for her. There was no doubt that her daughter adored him, soaking up his attention, kindness and— Abby paused. Love? Did Noah love her little girl? He had only met her a few short days ago, but the attention he lavished on her was such a healing balm for her sweet Charlotte—could she take that away from her?

Abby squeezed the scrubby and pulled the plug. The water swirled down the drain. Turning away from the sink, she smiled at Charlotte and Noah. "Thank you both."

"No need to thank us. Teamwork makes the dream work." Noah chuckled and lifted his hand, offering Charlotte a high five.

Her daughter beamed as she slapped her palm against his. "Mom, you, too."

Abby raised her palm, and Charlotte high-fived her. "Now you and Noah. The whole team."

Abby's eyes met his. Their palms touched. And when her lips curved into a smile, it carried wonder, relief, and joy that quietly rooted in her heart and sprouted something new—something much stronger.

True love.

"Can we teach Rosie and Briggs how to do that because they are a part of this family, too?"

A family?

"And once the puppies get older, we'll show them how to high-five as well, right, Noah?" Charlotte chimed in, obviously unaware of the look that passed between the two adults standing right next to her.

"You're too cute." Noah tussled Charlotte's hair. "Have I told you that before?"

"Yes, you did."

"But not today, right?" Noah asked her, his voice serious. "Because I would hate for you to think that I missed a day or I repeat myself too much."

Charlotte giggled and reached for his hand. "No, not today. But if you like, you can say it again, any time you think that I'm cute. I won't get upset." She tugged at his arm. "The doggies are waiting. Let's go."

Abby's heart filled with an overwhelming sense of love. She had loved Noah all those years ago. But watching him dote on her daughter, in a way no other person ever had, made her heart overflow. She took the dishcloth out of his hand. Abby smiled and gently swatted the cloth against his chest.

"You two better get going then. Don't let the mama wait any longer."

Noah followed Charlotte as she zoomed out of the house and ran toward the coach house.

"Slow down, Squirt." He sped up after her.

They entered the garage together. Briggs stood up, ready for his morning run. Rosie looked at them, her head resting on her paws.

"Doesn't she want to go for walk?" Charlotte asked, concern in her voice, as Noah opened the overhead garage door.

"I think she's getting pretty tired. The puppies are almost fully grown and her belly is getting heavy." He reached in and petted the mama-to-be. "Come on, girl, we can take it easy today."

Rosie lumbered to her feet. Noah knelt next to his dog and ran his finger over her belly, then looked up at his eager helper. "I think we might need to put that whelping box together fast."

Charlotte's eyes grew wide. "Are the puppies coming now?"

"Not at this moment, but very soon." He chuckled. "Let's take them out, make them breakfast, and then we'll build the box."

"Can Mom help?"

"Of course, if she wants to." How could he tell this little girl that having Abby join them was exactly what he had hoped for? *Thank You, Lord.*

Abby had surprised him this morning when she mentioned that she'd had no idea Natalie and Brad were married. But how would she? Their wedding was right after their college graduation, and by that time, Abby's parents had been dead for two years. And once Noah had rented her chalet, all communication from her hometown had ceased. "Briggs, fetch." Charlotte's voice rang out.

Her giggly laughter made him smile.

Noah's keen eyes settled on Rosie. His girl plopped on the grass, tongue hanging out.

"Charlotte, sweetheart, I think Rosie is too hot. Why don't we take the dogs inside the garage?"

"Can I make them kibble?"

"That's a great idea."

"And Rosie gets puppy food, even though she's not a puppy, right?"

Noah smiled. Did this girl ever forget anything? "Yep, you're absolutely right."

She stopped in the middle of the doorway, the dogs brushing past her in hurried anticipation of breakfast. "I'm so happy Rosie and Briggs get to stay here." Then she threw her arms around his waist. "And you, too."

Charlotte's open heart still surprised him. This child had been rejected by her own father, yet she was able to let God be the loving Father to her and bring forth healing, albeit via two rambunctious Vizslas.

"Me, too." He playfully tugged her ponytail.

Briggs whined, to remind them that breakfast was in order and he had been waiting.

"All right, let's feed these hungry dogs."

"Yes!" Her eyes glittered with excitement. Charlotte picked up the empty dishes off the floor and carefully measured out the granulated food. "Is this okay?" She tipped the bowls toward Noah.

"Perfect."

"Sit." Charlotte lifted her hand just like Noah showed her. The dogs obeyed.

"Good job," she praised them, then set the dishes in front of the impatient K-9s. "Not yet," she said as she straightened up. "Okay." She pointed at the food.

Both Vizslas rushed to the bowls and stuck their noses into the kibble. Rosie took a few pieces and dropped them on the garage floor. Briggs looked up, leaving the granules untouched.

"I forgot to add some love." Charlotte dramatically placed her palm on her forehead.

Noah chuckled. "Here." He passed her a shaker of powdered freeze-dried liver.

Charlotte squatted and shook the container over the dishes.

A fine dust of beef liver sprinkled over the dogs' breakfast. "Okay, you can try it now."

Both dogs stuck their noses into the offered food, and Briggs took a mouthful. Rosie picked up a few more pieces and dropped them on the floor again.

"Is Rosie not hungry today?" Charlotte looked up at Noah, worry in her eyes.

"I think she's getting ready to have the puppies."

"Today?"

Noah nodded silently, wondering how he was going to drive to the clinic, pick up the puppy and return to the chalet without missing the start of Rosie's labor. He was pretty sure today was the day the puppies would make their grand entrance, and he needed to be here for that.

The garage door opened, and Abby stuck her head in.

"How are you two doing?"

"Rosie isn't eating." Charlotte sounded worried.

"She isn't?" Abby stepped in and, much to Noah's surprise, bent down and petted his dog. "How are you, girl?" Her fingers ran down Rosie's back, then followed the curve of her large belly. "Do you think she's ready?" Abby looked up at Noah.

He nodded.

"Do you need help with the whelping box?"

"That would be great. It's folded over there." Noah pointed toward the back corner.

"I was thinking." Abby chewed on her bottom lip. "Would you feel comfortable with setting it up in the house? I think there's enough space in the laundry room."

Noah looked at her and smiled. How had she guessed that's exactly what he was hoping for? It would be much easier to control the room temperature inside the house, because the puppies needed to be kept warm for the first few days and the garage was pretty drafty. Plus, he needed to bring the rescue puppy from the clinic. Noah wasn't sure how Rosie would react to him. Any distractions during the labor and the first days of the puppies' lives could trigger fear. Dogs were naturally protective of their babies right after adelivery. Having Rosie nervous about another dog nearby wouldn't be a good situation.

"I'd really appreciate that."

"You could use the side entrance and come and go as you need. Would that work?"

"Absolutely."

"Mommy." Charlotte hugged her. "How did you know I was wishing for that?"

"Maybe I can read your mind," Abby teased. "Let's get the boards into the house and settle our big mama in so she can get used to everything."

Noah grabbed the four planks that would lock together to make a square whelping box, and Abby brought Rosie's blanket.

"Why don't you carry the dishes for her?" Noah said as he glanced over his shoulder and smiled at Charlotte. The dogs followed her.

"I will." She picked up Rosie's uneaten breakfast and the water dish. "But what will Briggs drink from?"

"I do have a spare bowl somewhere in my boxes. Once we settle Rosie, you could help me find it."

"For sure," she said and hopped toward the door. The trio, followed by the two dogs, marched across the driveway toward the house. They entered the laundry room through the side door.

They put together Rosie's whelping box as Briggs diligently sniffed all the parts. Abby placed the blanket inside. No one needed to tell Rosie to get in. As soon as the work was done, the dog climbed through the little door in one of the sides and settled down.

"I think she says she likes it," Charlotte said and leaned in to pet Rosie's head. The dog let out a low grunt. "Is she growling at me?"

"I don't think so," Noah assured her. "She's letting us know that it's time for her to nap. She'll sleep more than usual until the labor starts."

"Good night, Rosie." Charlotte bent down and kissed Rosie's head. "Have a good nap and call us when you're ready to have the puppies. Briggs, you come with me."

Noah smiled and opened the laundry room door. Charlotte stepped out first, with Briggs following right behind her. But before Abby had a chance to go out into the sunny morning, Noah gently reached for her arm.

She turned around, and his heart skipped a beat. Her eyes were so beautiful.

"Thank you," he whispered.

"You're most welcome," she said and lingered for a moment longer, locking her gaze with his. "It's the least I can do." She smiled. "Let's just pray that all goes well."

"I'm definitely praying," Noah agreed. "Not only for Rosie, but also for you and for that sweet girl of yours."

Tears glistened in Abby's eyes.

He pulled her a little closer and gently shut the door. Charlotte and Briggs would surely be fine if left in the house by themselves for a few moments.

"You know that God has never left you, don't you?" he whispered.

Abby nodded, a single tear sliding down her cheek.

Noah drew her closer. How long had he wished for one more chance with her, exactly like this one?

"God loves you, Abby. And so do I."

Chapter Twenty-Two

"Mommy! Look at this!" Charlotte's voice came loud and clear through the closed laundry room doors. "I taught Briggs a new trick."

Abby pulled away from Noah. A small smile came over her face.

"Okay, let me see." She reached for the doorknob.

"Before you go…" Noah rested his hand against the door.

She paused. Was he about to try to kiss her again? Her heart sped up. "Noah—"

"I know. It's not the right time for that." He smiled and cleared his throat.

She was glad they were on the same wavelength.

"What then?"

"I got the text. They finally got someone to sub for me this week. But I need to drive to the clinic and pick up the rescue puppy. Brad won't be able to come for the next two days, though, so—"

"Mommy, come."

"No problem." She smiled. "What's one more dog in the house?" She took a step back, not ready to be caught kissing Noah by that little spy outside the laundry room. "I'll keep an eye on Rosie, if that's what you're asking. And if anything happens, I'll call you."

"Thanks. I'll be back as soon as I can." Noah walked out the side door. She watched him head toward his red pickup.

He wore his old cowboy boots. How had she not noticed that earlier?

Abby's heart filled with hope. If she could ask God for a dad who would love her daughter and look after her, Noah would be the man she would choose. Now that she understood how immature she had been, letting their young love slip through her fingers, she hoped that God would restore all those years they had lost.

She opened the laundry room door and saw a tennis ball rolling down the hallway floor.

"Mommy," Charlotte called out to her. "Throw the ball back to me, Briggs loves chasing it."

Abby picked up the slobbery, bright green tennis ball.

"Honey, you need to take this outside."

"Okay, Mommy. Come!" she ordered the dog. Charlotte took the ball from her, grabbed her hand and pulled her toward the front door. "You have to see this."

"All right, but only for a few minutes. I want to do some more work in the house before Noah gets back."

They stepped into the sunshine. Briggs sat in front of Charlotte, waiting for her to throw the ball. The girl tossed it toward Abby. The excited dog rushed after it. Charlotte giggled. This was precisely what Abby had longed for. In this one sweet moment, Abby felt so much love it almost overwhelmed her. God had answered the prayers she'd uttered only a few short days ago. Her child was healing right before her eyes.

"Thank You," she whispered.

Briggs sat in front of her, his ball in his teeth. Abby chuckled.

"Good boy, give."

He lifted his face toward her, but when she reached for the ball, he gently pulled back. "You've got to give it to me if you want me to throw it."

The dog lifted his nose again. The scenario repeated.

"Charlotte, what does he want?"

"You have to pretend you're grabbing it and he'll play a tug-of-war, then let it go. Try it, Mom."

Abby laughed. "Did you teach him that, too?"

"Yep," her daughter said with a cute hint of pride in her voice. "I'll teach him a lot more tricks, because he's smart. And then I will teach the puppies."

Briggs finally let go of the ball and Abby tossed it toward her daughter. The dog followed his toy with so much enthusiasm that Abby wished for some of that energy.

"How many puppies do you think Rosie will have?" Charlotte called out as the ball flew through the air.

"Hard to tell. Did you ask Noah?"

"He said he thinks five, but there could be more. I told him she will have ten."

"You still think that?"

"Yes."

Briggs snatched the bouncing ball with his teeth. Then he sat in front of her, his irises wide with excitement. "Did you see that, Mommy?" Charlotte's voice was full of enthusiasm.

"Sweetie, I should go make sure Rosie is okay."

"I want to check, too, but what about Briggs?"

"Why don't we let him in through the front door into the hallway? The laundry room is shut. Then we'll walk around the house to the outside door and peek in through the glass." Abby hoped with all her heart that the dog wouldn't go into active labor before Noah got back.

Noah drove down the mountain thinking about Abby. Rosie was so close to having the puppies, he would have to rush back. Hopefully, there were no surprises waiting for him at the clinic. Noah parked in his designated spot near the Hope Rock Veterinary Clinic entrance. He got out of his truck and walked in.

"Dr. Noah." Cindy frowned. "Didn't you get my message? You got this whole week off."

"I'm just stopping by to pick up the puppy. My brother messaged me, he is coming by to pick him up today. Rosie is about to give birth, and I've got to get back up the mountain as soon as possible."

"Of course." Cindy stepped out from behind her desk and walked with him into the second examination room on the left. "He's been doing well, but honestly, we don't know what to do next. I think he needs more space."

"You're right, of course. Brad has a place for him at the no-kill shelter. I'm positive he'll get adopted out in no time."

"That's a relief. He definitely tugs at your heartstrings, don't you, little guy?" Cindy scratched behind the puppy's ear.

"Let me grab a crate and we'll be on our way back up the mountain."

Just then, the phone in the reception area rang. "I'll let it go to voicemail. This little one needs one more snuggle before I let him go." She kissed the pup's face. "You be a good boy now." She carefully placed the puppy inside the blanket-lined pet carrier Noah held out to her.

"Sorry to cut this short, but I've got to go."

"Of course." The phone at the front desk rang again. "Give Rosie a hug for me," Cindy chirped as she rushed to her desk. "I'll be thinking of her."

"Thank you," Noah said as he walked briskly toward the front door.

"Hello, Hope Rock Veterinary Clinic, could you hold please?" Cindy pressed a button and set the receiver atop a pile of papers. "Let me get that for you." She pulled at the doorknob. "And text us some pictures. The entire clinic is excited about the puppies."

"Will do," Noah said and rushed toward his truck, not wanting the little dog to get cold.

With the pet carrier securely buckled in the passenger seat, Noah drove back up the mountain, the little puppy slowly drifting off to sleep.

* * *

As Noah's truck reached the top of the driveway, he smiled. Brad's truck was already parked in front of the coach house. When they talked last, they had agreed that he'd come on Wednesday, not today. Noah pulled in and reached for the pet carrier.

"All right, let's see how this will play out, little one."

The tiny dog woke up and squinted at him.

Noah walked briskly and saw that the door to the garage was slightly ajar. Brad had been here before, so he knew there was a loft apartment above. Noah set the pet carrier down on the workbench and rushed upstairs.

"Hey, bro." Brad pushed himself off the old recliner. "It's been a while." He crossed the space between them and wrapped his arms around Noah's shoulders. "How are you?"

"Hi!" Natalie rushed over. "How is my auxiliary husband?" she kidded, giving Noah a side hug. This was an ongoing joke between the three of them, as he and Brad were identical twins. They had fun seeing the confused expressions on people's faces before they realized that Noah and Brad were two men, not just one.

"What a surprise! I had no idea you were coming too. So nice to see you." He hugged his sister-in-law back. Noah cleared his throat. "You look like you are about to pop," he teased her. "But listen, we need to talk."

"Had something happened?"

"No. Nothing to worry about. Abby is back in town."

"I wondered about that, after seeing another car in the driveway. How is she?"

"Well…" Noah looked at his brother and scratched the back of his neck.

Brad's eyes grew wide. "I remember that look." He chuckled. "Don't tell me, bro—are you back together?"

Natalie looked at her husband, then back at Noah.

"Really?" A wide smile broke on her face.

"I hope so," Noah said sheepishly.

"Hmm," Brad grunted. "That may complicate things a little."

"What do you mean?"

"I saw Dr. Weishoff this morning. He asked me to pass along a message—he's finally retiring. Said you'd want to know since you've had your eye on that River Run practice for years."

Noah's eyebrows shot up.

"You're kidding. Retiring? At River Run?"

"No joke. He's putting the whole thing up for sale—the clinic and the house. Told me you should jump on it before word gets out." Brad grinned.

"That's…everything I've been waiting for."

"But what about Abby?" Natalie gently touched his arm.

"I don't know." Noah rubbed the back of his neck.

"You don't know? What do you mean, Bro?" Brad sounded a little concerned.

"What he means—" Abby's voice cut into their conversation as she came up the stairs "—is that we are still sorting things out." She stopped at the top of the stairs. Her eyes found Noah's. "River Run? That would mean leaving Hope Rock."

"Abby, I don't know. This is a bit of a surprise—this has been my dream for a long time. But it would mean," he searched her eyes. "It would mean not being here."

Abby's expression hardened.

"And that's okay." Her voice caught. "Really," she added as if she needed to assure herself. "We don't want to stand in your way, Noah."

"Abby…"

"We can talk later, Noah," she cut off their conversation, then turned toward Natalie and Brad. Abby mustered a smile. "I'm so glad to see you. I've so much to apologize for to the two of you."

Chapter Twenty-Three

"Hey there, stranger," Brad said to her, with a hint of a smile on his face. "Come over here. How are you?"

"Getting better every day," Abby responded as she walked toward him, her arm stretched out, offering him a handshake. He still looked so much like his twin brother, wearing old jeans and an olive-green T-shirt, except for the beard and the crew cut.

Her mind was swirling with thoughts. Was Noah going to move to River Run? He'd said that practice was everything he had been waiting for—just when she thought she could trust him. Abby suppressed her tears. She needed to make this reunion short—there would be plenty of time to sort this out and catch up with her friends after the puppies were born. Charlotte was sitting next to Rosie. She refused to leave her side, so Abby had no other choice but to run out herself to fetch Noah. From what she could tell, the puppies were almost here. Noah needed to come. Now. Abby's jumbled emotions had to wait.

"Oh, come on." Brad waved her hand away and wrapped her in a big hug. "So glad to see you."

Natalie took a step closer, waiting for her turn. Abby looked at her former best friend over Brad's shoulder and smiled through her tears. Natalie was very pregnant, and Abby wondered why she would take a five-hour drive through the mountains this close to her due date. Aside from her large belly, Natalie hadn't changed much, still tying her black hair into a messy bun atop her head. Abby let go of Brad and hurried toward her long-lost friend. Natalie's face was one huge smile, her green eyes brimming with tears. Of course, Abby couldn't be rude and rush off, so she silently prayed that Rosie would hold on for a few more minutes and that Charlotte would be okay. Abby owed her best friend so much more than a warm hug.

"I'm so sorry for disappearing on you all those years ago without as much as a word. Can you ever forgive me?"

Natalie hugged her. "There's nothing to forgive. I'm so glad you're back in Hope Rock."

She'd missed this girl—a married woman now. She'd missed her best friend's wedding and so much more. It was only just last night that Abby had finally found the courage to open her heart to Noah. Would Brad and Natalie feel the same?

She pulled out of her friend's embrace. "I—" she stammered. "I've made a terrible mistake—well, several of them—"

"Haven't we all?" Natalie smiled. "Why don't we let bygones be bygones and start all over again?" She reached for Abby's hand. "You look like you've tortured yourself long enough."

Abby smiled through her tears.

A whining sound carried up to the loft.

"Noah?" She shot him a look. "What was that?"

"The puppy must be getting hungry." He walked toward the stairs.

"You also need to check on Rosie," Abby called after him.

"Maybe you should let us take care of the puppy and go," Natalie said as she rushed down the stairs, following Noah.

Abby looked at Brad. "There's so much to apologize for, but I've got to go now. Can we talk later?"

"Sure. After you." Brad motioned to the stairs. "Glad to see you back in town. Noah's never been the same since that summer," he said under his breath as they descended. "All work. No fun. But I see that spark back in his eyes. I hope you can stay, because—"

Abby glanced back at him over her shoulder.

"I'm so sorry—about everything," she whispered as they reached the garage.

"Oh, my word," Natalie said, her excited voice filling the space. "He is so cute."

"Brad, you know what to do with this puppy better than me, so please check him over. Abby and I need to get back to the house. Charlotte must be worried."

"Who is Charlotte?" Natalie asked.

"Abby's daughter," Noah said. "We have a lot of catching up to do. Wait till you meet her."

"All right, let us take care of the puppy and you go," Brad said, reaching into the pet carrier. "We can all chat later."

Noah caught Abby's gaze. She was already standing by the door, impatient, silently urging him on.

"Go, go." Brad motioned to his brother.

"Thanks," Noah said under his breath as he and Abby rushed back to the cabin.

Walking across the driveway, Noah and Abby entered the laundry room through the back door.

"I'm so glad you're here." Charlotte looked up, her eyes wide.

The girl had squeezed herself into the whelping box, holding Rosie's head in her lap. Her hand slowly traced the dog's back.

"She's whimpering."

"And that's okay." Noah squatted. "How are you, girl?" He patted Rosie's head. "You have the best nurse in the world here." He looked up at Charlotte. "Thank you for keeping her company. It shouldn't take much longer. We need to get some old towels."

"I'll go get some," Abby said, rushing off.

Noah hesitated. What else could he ask Charlotte to do?

"I need you to get out of the box now. Rosie will need more room as the puppies come." He reached for the girl's hand and helped her get up.

She climbed out of the whelping box and then tiptoed toward the door.

"I'll help Mom look for the towels," she whispered.

"Thank you for remembering to be so very quiet." Noah glanced up at her, his heart overflowing with love.

God, please help us. Help Rosie have a good delivery. Help the three of us find a way forward. I'm not sure I can let go of these two.

His gaze dropped to Rosie. "Okay, girl. We're ready."

Rosie looked at him, her brown eyes trusting. Noah petted her and settled on the floor next to the whelping box.

The door cracked open, and Charlotte stuck her head through the opening. "We got the towels," she whispered.

"Great. So, this is what is going to happen. As the puppies are born, I will look them over, then let Rosie lick them off. That's very important, so she bonds with them, but as she delivers her next puppy, I will pass the licked one to you."

Abby stepped into the room.

He looked at her, relieved that she was here.

"How can I help?" she asked, her voice calm.

"I need you to dry them off with a towel." He held Abby's gaze. "Then pass each one to Charlotte."

Abby nodded.

"What should I do?" Charlotte asked.

"Wrap them in the towel, hold them for a little bit. Use your pinkie finger to gently touch their ears and nose, so that they learn that we won't hurt them. Then pass the puppies back to me. I'll give them a collar and you can note the color next to each name on your list. Then, I'll place them in the whelping box, so they are close to their mom and can start nursing."

"How many will there be?" Abby asked.

"I could make out five spines on the X-ray, but it all depends on how they were positioned. Sometimes we don't get to see them all." Both of them leaned over the edge of the whelping box holding their breath in awe, as the first puppy arrived.

"Here we are," Noah said, his voice gentle and soothing. "What a good girl." He picked up the little baby dog and passed it to the mama. She vigorously licked her firstborn, cleaning its face and then progressing down the little body.

Abby's heart swelled as the tiny, wriggling puppy let out their first cries, Noah's steady hands guiding it into life. She wanted to laugh, to rejoice—but the sound caught in her throat. Because even as she watched him, tender and sure, the thought struck her with piercing clarity: River Run. He could walk away, start fresh somewhere else, just as her walls were finally crumbling. And the truth she'd tried so hard to ignore pressed in—she wasn't just grateful for his help.

She was falling in love with him.

Charlotte let out a squeal of excitement, then clasped both hands over her mouth, most likely trying not to startle Rosie or the puppy. Noah caressed Rosie. He straightened up and reached for one of the tiny collars.

"How about green for the first collar?" He looked at excited Charlotte.

"Is it a boy or a girl?"

Noah slowly reached into the whelping box and checked the puppy. "A boy," he said quietly.

"Green is okay." Her fingers disappeared in the back pocket of her jeans. Charlotte pulled out a list, then a crayon. "His name is Pretzel."

"Of course." Noah glanced back inside the whelping box. Abby's chest tightened at the sight, sweetness and sorrow colliding. How could she bear to explain to her little girl that Noah's place in their world might only be temporary? "Get ready," he said to Abby. Her eyes were big, glistening with tears of joy and sorrow.

"Are you okay?"

She pushed tomorrow's worries to the back of her mind and let herself enjoy the present moment.

"I've never seen anything like this," she whispered.

The process continued. An hour later, there were nine puppies.

"I think we may be done," he said. "Time to take a little break."

"Shouldn't we wait for the last puppy?" Charlotte asked.

"Honey," Noah said, "this is it. There are nine of them, which is a lot, don't you think?"

"There should be ten." Charlotte seemed to be convinced.

"Well, nine might be our number." Noah smiled. "I think all of us deserve a little break."

"But we are still missing Cinnamon."

Noah looked to Abby for help.

"Do we just leave them all here?" Abby asked.

"They'll go to sleep. Rosie is exhausted, and the babies are, too, so everything is the way it should be."

"Can I stay with them?" Charlotte said.

"If your mom says it's okay, I don't see why not."

Perhaps this would be a good time to have a chat with Abby over a cup of fresh coffee. Noah was thankful that Natalie and Brad didn't seem to be in any rush to leave. He would hate for them to drive back without a proper visit. It was time to clear up the high school prom mix-up, so he and Abby could move on—on to the future he so hoped was within his reach.

"Would you like some coffee?" he asked, walking toward the kitchen.

"I would love one." Abby was right behind him.

Noah had just started making coffee when suddenly the door flew open.

"Noah! Another puppy is coming! I don't know what to do!"

"Another puppy?"

"Yes, the tenth puppy!"

Noah set down the coffee can and rushed to the laundry room. "Honey, I need you to stay out here," he said as he stepped inside the laundry room.

"Why? What's wrong?"

"Nothing. Everything will be fine." He tousled Charlotte's hair, then closed the door.

Abby followed them both, her heart pounding in her chest. There was so much going on. The unexpected reunion, Noah's constant presence, Charlotte's obvious infatuation with him, the puppies—but what weighed down on her the most were her unexpected guests, hopefully still waiting at the loft. She owed them an explanation. Abby leaned into the doorway, only to see Noah holding a tenth tiny puppy.

"Is the last puppy okay?" Charlotte pushed through the open door past her mom.

Noah shot Abby a look. "Could you go get Brad? Fast. I need his help."

Charlotte gripped Abby's hand.

Abby momentarily locked her gaze with Noah's. Was he trying to save the puppy or protect Charlotte from heartbreak? His eyes were full of softness and love. Then she understood. He was trying to do both.

"Charlotte, run ahead, I'll be right behind you."

The girl sprinted outside.

"I'll pray that the little one makes it."

"Thank you." Noah focused on the tiny puppy in his hands.

Abby followed her daughter to the loft, whispering a prayer under her breath.

"Brad," she called out, seeing him open the back of his truck.

"Noah needs help saving the last puppy," Charlotte called out. She stopped, momentarily forgetting the crisis. She stared at Brad. "You look just like Noah."

"I know, sweetheart, I get that a lot," Brad said, as he sprinted toward the house.

"Mom?"

Abby reached for her daughter and wrapped her in her arms.

"Who is that?"

"Noah's twin brother. He also works with animals. You will get to meet him properly as soon as—"

"Will the puppy be okay?" Charlotte interrupted, tears in her eyes.

"What's happening?" Natalie asked as she walked down the stairs from the loft, into the sunlight.

"Noah needs help with one of the puppies," Abby said.

Natalie looked at Charlotte, then met Abby's eyes.

"Let's pray." She reached for her old friend with one hand and for Charlotte's with the other. Abby filled her lungs with a deep breath. Natalie's offer to pray right there gave her a renewed sense of hope.

"Dear Lord," Natalie began. "Thank You for this day and thank You for Rosie and her puppies. We ask You to have mercy on the little one and help him or her live. Thank You for Noah and Brad. If anyone can save this little one, it's the two of them. Thank You for Abby and her daughter."

"Charlotte," the little girl chimed in.

Abby opened her eyes. A smile curled up the corners of Natalie's lips.

"Yes, Lord, thank You for Charlotte and her mom, Abby," Natalie continued, "for giving Rosie a safe place to have the puppies and to be loved and cared for. We trust that You hear our prayers. And while we're talking to You, I ask you to forgive us for all the hurtful things we've done to others, whether they've been intentional or accidental, or just plain dumb. You're the God of love and restoration, and I ask You to touch our hearts and make them whole. Amen."

"Can you say *dumb* when you pray?" Charlotte looked at Abby.

"Well, if you do something really dumb, I guess you could."

Charlotte glanced at Natalie. "I hope God heard you."

"I'm sure He did. I'm Natalie, by the way." She stretched out her arm. Charlotte accepted the offered hand.

"Are you Noah's friend?"

"I married his brother, so I guess that would make us friends and family."

"Charlotte," Noah's voice interrupted the introductions. "Come meet Cinnamon."

The girl's eyes grew wide with wonder.

"God did hear us!" She sprinted toward Noah. "Is it a boy or a girl?"

"A girl."

"I knew it!" Charlotte pumped the air.

Noah's laughter filled the surrounding space.

"Well, come on in." He walked her back into the laundry room. "Cinnamon needs cuddles."

Abby watched them disappear around the corner, then turned toward her high school friend. "Natalie," she said, her voice wavering. "I—"

Natalie reached for her hand. "If you're trying to apologize, I need to do that first. I'm so sorry I didn't try harder to reach out to you. After you left town, Brad and I tried to be there for Noah, not understanding why you dumped him."

Abby looked up.

Dumped him?

"Maybe that was the wrong choice of words." Natalie held her gaze. "After you left, we were so lost and confused. Neither of us understood what had happened—" Natalie's voice caught. "I was so worried, wondering if something happened at your house, but your parents were such good people." Natalie's eyes filled with tears. "And then you came back for the funeral. Married."

Tears rolled down Abby's cheeks. Even if she apologized a

thousand times, she wouldn't be able to fix this. But she had to try.

"I'm so sorry for hurting you and Brad." Now, tears streamed down her face. "Hurting Noah." She swiped at them. "Wrecking our friendship and the beautiful thing Noah and I shared. I—" Abby could no longer speak. A torrent of past hurts, bitter memories and heavy burdens suddenly came to the surface of her heart. She reached for her friend and wrapped her in a tight hug. "I missed you so much."

"I missed you, too." Natalie clung to her best friend. "So very much."

And in that embrace, the years of silence melted away, and the sweet friendship that had once been broken found a new promise of hope and healing. Even if Noah chose River Run, Abby's heart brimmed with thankfulness. She had her friend back, and that alone felt like a gift she didn't deserve. Whatever tomorrow held, today was a piece of grace she would never forget.

Chapter Twenty-Four

The rest of the day was a complete whirlwind. Abby's heart was overflowing with love as she kept checking on Rosie and her new family. She had never seen anything as cute as ten identical Vizsla puppies, little potato-size bundles of fawn-colored fur, neatly tucked in around Rosie. The proud mama dog grinned at her, tongue lolling, every time Abby stuck her head into the laundry room to make sure all was well.

Charlotte was bubbling with energy, busy keeping an eye on the rescue puppy, showing Briggs her room and quizzing Brad and Natalie. Abby made her settle down for a few moments, allowing her to let Briggs cuddle up with her on the bed as she read her favorite picture book to him.

As the house quieted down, Abby walked into the living room, coffee in hand, and sank onto the sofa opposite Noah's chair.

"What a day." She exhaled, took a sip of coffee and looked up at him. "I went from zero to thirteen dogs of our own in less than twenty-four hours." She laughed. "Somehow, I still can't believe that."

"Neither can I," he chuckled. "Thank you for letting Rosie stay in your laundry room. I'll do my best to get the coach house garage in shape this week so we can move there."

"There's no rush. I quite like having her here. It makes it easier to pop in and make sure the puppies are doing well."

"I'll remind you of this conversation in about two weeks, when the puppies realize there is a world beyond the whelping box. Here, let me show you some pictures of my last litter."

Noah got up, pulled the phone from the back pocket of his jeans and sat next to Abby. He tapped the screen. A video of a pack of tiny dogs made Abby laugh.

"I'm telling you, they are pretty smart. Here, look at the hole they dug up in the yard. I filled it every day and they started a new one the next morning, trying to get out of the enclosure."

A video of Noah rolling on the grass, play-wrestling with eight puppies, began to play. Abby's heart filled with so much love that she almost blurted out the words she wasn't ready to say. Yet.

"Wait till Charlotte sees this. She'll insist that we keep them all."

"About that." Noah's voice grew a little serious. "I want to ask you something."

"What is it?" A little cloud of worry threatened to cast a shadow on this wonderful day. Was this when he would tell her that he had decided to move with the puppies to River Run? How would she break the news to Charlotte?

"I usually find homes for them when they are about ten weeks old, but I was thinking. And that is only if you would agree to it."

"Noah, tell me already." She motioned with her hand for him to speak faster.

"I'd like to keep them longer and train them as emotional support dogs."

"In the house?" Abby asked.

"Of course not," Noah chuckled. "You can't let ten Vizsla puppies loose in here, they would demolish the entire place in minutes."

"So, where would you like to train them?" River Run?

"I was thinking I could install a temporary kennel in the

garage of the coach house, once they are weaned. That would give them direct access to the outside, and I would be able to keep an eye on them at night, since they would be right below my apartment."

Abby placed her fingers over her lips. Was Noah telling her, in a roundabout way, that he would like to stay at the loft long-term? Her heart sped up. She should ask him but wasn't sure if he would agree. She worried about his long commute to the Hope Rock vet clinic, but that was before his brother mentioned River Run.

"What about Charlotte?"

Noah's eyebrows knitted in confusion.

"She'll be pestering you day and night, especially if you keep the puppies for a few months. You know how enthusiastic she is. She loves your dogs."

"Well—" Noah grinned mischievously. "Charlotte is a part of my grand plan, if you would be okay with that."

"What grand plan?" Was he going to suggest she and Charlotte move to River Run? And what if he didn't?

"I would like to train some of these pups to work with children. Charlotte would be a perfect trainer for that."

Abby was confused. Her heart was positively overflowed with joy, yet the icy grip of fear and insecurity crushed her spirit.

"She would be over the moon as soon as you tell her, but—"

Briggs ran into the room.

"Tell me what?" Charlotte followed right behind him.

"Noah has something special in mind, but looking at the time, we'd better start thinking about dinner. Brad and Natalie should have the rescue puppy settled by now. They will be staying the night in the loft. Maybe you could run up and get them."

"Can Briggs help, Noah?"

"Of course." He reached out and gently tugged at her ponytail. "Squirt."

The girl ran out of the house, Briggs right at her heels.

Watching Noah's gentle way of drawing Charlotte in—how easily he made her feel seen—filled Abby with a rush of joy tangled with dread. The sweetness of hope soured by the thought that River Run might steal him away. Just as her heart was daring to open again, the possibility of losing him threatened to crush it all over again. How could she bear to let him back into her heart if he was only going to leave?

Maybe it was all the excitement, or the emotional roller coaster of the day, or just the sight of a beautiful, sweet girl enjoying the simple things in life, like a litter of cute puppies, but Noah suddenly felt emotional. Life was turning out the way he had dreamed of for so long. Abby sat next to him, watching his puppy videos, laughing at the little dogs' shenanigans. A new litter of healthy Vizslas rested only a few steps away. His brother and Natalie had rekindled their friendship with the woman he loved—he took in a deep breath and let it out slowly.

Thank You, Lord.

His prayer, though only a whisper, was straight from his overflowing heart. This perfect moment was an answer to his prayers.

"Are you okay?" Abby looked at him, a touch of concern on her face.

"Yes," he said and smiled reassuringly. "More than okay." He reached for her hand. "I'm happy."

"So am I." She squeezed his fingers. "But I'm also a little worried."

"About what?"

Should she bring up River Run? But that would be a much deeper conversation, and there was no time for that now. Abby drew a deep breath.

"Well, we have a full house, and I'm not sure what I can rustle up to eat. Besides a couple of tomatoes and a head of lettuce, the fridge is pretty empty."

"Ahh." He grinned. "Noah to the rescue."

She chuckled.

"There's a secret stash of frozen burger patties and buns in the garage freezer. There wasn't enough space for them in my condo fridge."

"But that's just perfect. Why don't you fire up the grill? I'll slice up the tomatoes and wash the lettuce in the meantime and perhaps we can have a bonfire after supper and make s'mores. Charlotte's never had one."

"Well—" Noah pushed to his feet, then reached for her hand and helped her up. "It's about time we fixed that."

Chapter Twenty-Five

Abby welcomed the opportunity to share the kitchen with Natalie, even if only for one evening. There was so much she wanted to know. She had a million questions.

"Here, if you don't mind—" She passed Natalie a knife and a cutting board. "If you could slice the tomatoes, that would be great."

"For sure," Natalie said.

"Tell me about your daughter," Abby asked.

"Her name is Edie, and she's five."

"And when is this one coming?" Abby pointed with her chin toward Natalie's belly.

"Six more weeks and we will be parents of three."

"What?" Abby beamed. "You're expecting twins?"

"Yes, we are. Two girls."

Abby set down the head of lettuce and hugged her friend. "I'm so happy for you."

Natalie beamed. Then she gave her a meaningful look. "So… what's the story between you and Noah? You know, I haven't seen him this happy since the summer you left."

Guilt threatened to suck all the happiness out of the moment.

Natalie placed her hand on her forearm.

"I'm not trying to make you feel bad, Abby. Honest. All I'm saying is that he—"

"Yes?" Abby looked at her, hope rising in her heart.

"Well, he hasn't dated anyone since you left town. Not even after you got married. We were all worried about him, to be honest."

Tears prickled in Abby's eyes as she picked up the head of lettuce and cut it in half.

"I had wondered about that." She reached for a paper towel. "And how are Noah's brothers and your sister? Sorry, I lost track of everyone."

Natalie's expression softened, a quiet smile tugging at her lips.

"They're all doing well. But I think Noah's been waiting for more than just time to pass—if you know what I mean."

Abby looked at her. Of course. He had been waiting for Dr. Weishoff to retire, so he could take over his practice. She dabbed at her eyes with the paper towel, her heart both aching and strangely lighter. She was happy for him. This was something he had wanted for a long time and she wouldn't stand in his way.

Just before Noah declared the hamburgers were done, Brad went back to the coach house to make sure the rescue puppy was doing well. As soon as he returned, everyone took a chair at the big dining room table and dug in.

Noah looked around the room, his heart full of gratitude. This was precisely what he had wished for. Abby glowed with happiness, deep in conversation with Natalie, Brad's plate was overflowing with food. Charlotte was sneaking bits of hamburger to Briggs under the table, while coaxing funny twin stories out of Brad. Noah's eyes wandered back to the woman of his dreams. He marveled at how little she had changed since that summer over a decade ago. She was beautiful. The warmth of her smile lit up the room. The cadence of her voice made his heart sing. He would have to call Dr. Weishoff and tell him that as much as he appreciated the offer, his plans had changed.

"Excuse me," he said and stood up. "I'd better check on Rosie."

"Can I come?" Charlotte asked.

"Not this time." Noah smiled at her. "Why don't you and Briggs finish that hamburger—" he winked at her "—and then you can wish the puppies good night just before they tuck in."

"Okay, Noah," she nodded and took a huge bite of her burger.

"Slow down, Charlotte," Abby said. "I don't want you to choke."

"Okay, Mommy," Charlotte said with a mouth full of food.

Natalie and Brad laughed.

"I'll be right back," Noah said, walking toward the laundry room. If the conversation kept up, perhaps no one would notice him leaving the house. He sneaked a peek into the laundry room. Rosie and the puppies were sleeping. Then he carefully opened the front door and walked across the driveway to the coach house.

As he passed the heating lamp keeping the rescue puppy warm, he smiled at the sleeping little dog. His brother would surely find him a good home. He sped up the stairs, taking them two at a time. He'd better hurry before anyone started to wonder what was taking him this long.

He crossed the space in a few quick strides and reached for the nightstand door. It caught, and he had to shut it, then try to open it again. Noah reached inside, rummaging through the contents until he felt the small box. With his heart in his throat, he flipped the velvet lid open. The tiny diamond caught the last ray of the setting sun and sparkled—igniting the hope buried deep in his heart. Of course, he would get Abby something a little more substantial when the time came, but this ring had always been meant for her and no one else.

He put the box into his pocket. Rushing back to the house, his heart thudded in his ears. He had dinner to finish, a fire to start, s'mores to make—and a question to ask.

Chapter Twenty-Six

The low flames of the crackling fire reflected in Noah's eyes. He leaned forward, elbows resting on his knees. There was an empty space next to him on the bench. Her dad had made them from rough logs and placed them around the stone-lined fire pit—a welcoming circle with enough space for everyone. Should she get up and walk over? Or did Noah need a little time to recover from all the excitement of this day? Abby pulled the blanket tighter around her shoulders and took another sip of her hot chocolate. The Valentine's Day mug, firmly gripped in her right hand, anchored her. She looked over the low flames at the wonderful man sitting opposite her. Her heart was so full of bright love, she imagined its sparks flying up, toward the star-studded sky as prayers of gratitude.

It had been a long day and Charlotte had finally fallen asleep, but not before she convinced them that Briggs absolutely had to sleep in her bed, since Rosie had all ten puppies to keep her company, but he was all by himself. What were a few dog hairs in comparison to the boundless love the dog lavished on her daughter?

Brad and Natalie were also in bed in the loft. Abby was grateful they had decided to stay the night. There was this new kind of lightness in her heart, now that Natalie and she were talking once again. It had been so refreshing to chat by the fire tonight, catching up on life while roasting marshmallows. She couldn't wait to meet Brad and Natalie's daughter, Edie.

"What are you thinking about?" Noah asked in a husky tone.

"This day. It turned out just perfect."

He looked like he wanted to say something but then changed his mind. Instead, he got up and walked toward her.

"Scooch over," he said and sat next to her on the very same bench they used to snuggle on together as teenagers in love.

"You look a little worried." Noah playfully bumped her with his shoulder.

"If only I could turn back time," she sighed, "I would do so many things differently."

He moved a little closer. "You would?"

"In a heartbeat."

"In that case—" he smiled "—I've something I would like to ask you."

She looked at him. The tenderness in his eyes was so sweet, her heart swelled. "What?"

"I was wondering…" A sheepish smile turned up the corners of his mouth. "If you would be my girlfriend."

Suddenly, Abby felt eighteen again, sitting next to the kindest boy she had ever met. Only he was no longer a boy, but a wonderful, kind and handsome man offering his heart to her once more. Her throat grew thicker as tears of happiness fought their way to the surface, yet there still was one more unresolved issue that prevented her from fully embracing this moment.

"Noah—" Her words caught.

His eyes were full of questions.

"I—"

He pulled away.

"Abby—" Now his words seemed unable to pass his lips. "Have I misunderstood?"

"No." She breathed the word, struggling to hold back tears. "It's just that I don't think I can do a long-distance relationship."

He looked stunned.

"Noah, as wonderful as this is," she waved her hand in the space between them, "I have Charlotte to think about. She already has a man in her life who lives miles away, and whose absence crushed her heart."

"I don't understand what—" His eyebrows knitted tightly together.

She turned to face him. "Noah, you are a wonderful man, and I don't want to stand in the way of your success. I would never do that to you."

He tilted his head, obviously still confused.

"River Run?" she offered.

Noah chuckled, then shook his head. "Abby, if you think that I would trade this," he copied her hand motion, "for a clinic and a big empty house, then you still don't understand what really matters to me." He reached for her hand. "So, to make things perfectly clear, let me ask you again, would you be my girlfriend?"

"I would love to," she whispered.

Noah brought her hand it to his lips. And when he kissed her fingers, his eyes still on hers, a thought flashed through her mind. Never had she thought that one short prayer would have the power to break through all the pain and unhappiness, the regrets of lost friendships and time. This was where she needed to be. Right next to the handsome Dr. Ross, her Noah. Abby felt as if a heavy load of bricks had slipped off her shoulders.

She let out a slow breath. Tiny embers floated up from the crackling fire. The crickets sang in the forest behind them and the clear sky was full of millions of stars. How could she have left all this beauty behind? *Lord, thank You for being the God of second chances.* Abby shifted closer to the man still holding her hand and leaned on him, his arm wrapped around her shoulder.

His warmth was the comfort she so needed. Abby's shoulders relaxed as she nestled against his side. "Thank you for giving me a second chance, Noah." He was the man she was meant to share her life with. She was sure of that now. Noah had forgiven her for breaking his heart and leaving without an explanation. He had put up with her terrible attitude, coldness and stubbornness. He'd given her space and time to heal. His presence still stirred such feelings of love in her heart that she was powerless to deny them any longer.

Abby knew he loved her, and she loved him in return.

"Noah." She said his name softly.

"Hmm," he murmured into her hair.

"Thank you for being so loving. You have been nothing but wonderful to me and Charlotte—" She paused, gathering her courage. "And I've repaid you with coldness and rejection."

"Abby—"

"Please, let me finish. And you forgave me for the years of silence. I keep asking God to heal me, but I've realized I've been my own worst enemy. By clinging to my anger, I undid all that God was trying to work out in my life."

She sipped her hot chocolate, taking a moment to organize her thoughts.

"Thank you for praying for me."

"Always." He kissed her temple. "The past is behind us, if we choose to let go of it," Noah said in a hushed tone.

Abby nodded.

"All we have is this moment. And the hope for our future."

Hope.

Did she dare to hope once again for happiness, acceptance and love? She set her mug on the ground. This was her chance to set things right. She was sure that she could take the first step on the new path that had just opened before her.

"I love you," she whispered, searching his eyes.

Noah kissed her hair, then let go of her hand and touched her cheek. He lifted it toward his face.

"I love you, too, Abby."

His lips gently touched hers. Abby felt the oceans of grief drain away from her. She knew that with this man by her side, she could let go of all past hurts and disappointments and believe once again that God had her future in His hands. All she needed to do was trust Him.

"Noah," she whispered when their lips parted. "I want to thank you for not giving up on me."

"I could never give up on you. You are the love of my life." He let go of her hand and wrapped her in a tight embrace. He kissed her with such tenderness and love, she could no longer hold back.

And then Noah let go of her and got up, a strange look in his eyes. She tried to stand, wondering if he was ready to extinguish the fire and call it a night, but he lifted his hand and motioned her to stay seated.

Nervous jitters ran through Noah. Was this too soon? Would asking her right now spoil this perfect day? But he had been waiting all his life to do this. He cleared his throat.

"Abby—" His voice caught. "I've another question for you. I was planning to ask you this right after high school graduation, but I never got the chance."

Her eyes were on him, reflecting the glow of the smoldering fire.

"I promised myself that I would wait as long as it took." He shifted his weight. "And prayed that my chance would come. I had no idea you would go through so much heartache before I got to do that, and I'm truly sorry. I should have known better than to take a no for an answer then, but we were so young, thinking we knew everything, yet we knew nothing about life."

He caught her gaze, hoping that his eyes were telling the rest of the story, for he wasn't sure if he had enough courage to say the rest. If she said no, his life would implode right there and then.

Abby took a deep breath, as if ready to interrupt him. He gently lifted his right hand.

"Please," he pleaded with her. If she interrupted him, he would most likely lose his nerve. He took a deep breath of the chilly mountain air. "And I would never forgive myself if I let the moment pass me by without asking what I should have asked all those years ago."

He reached into his pocket and took a knee.

Abby took a sharp breath and covered her lips with both of her hands. Her eyes glittered with unshed tears, dancing in the last bits of the amber light.

Noah bowed his head as if searching for courage or perhaps whispering a word of prayer. When he looked back at her, his eyes, too, were filled with tears, glistening in the light of the rising moon.

He smiled. It was the same charming smile that had stolen her heart all those years ago.

"Abby Burns. Now that you're my girlfriend—" He paused. "Again."

A chuckle escaped her.

"I have a question for you."

He opened his hand and held a small velvet box in front of her.

A tear slid down her cheek.

Noah opened the box with his other hand, and the stone set in the center of the perfect ring caught a ray of moonlight.

"Abby, I've loved you all my life. Will you marry me?"

She closed her eyes, letting the wave of pure joy wash over her. When she opened them again, Noah was staring at her, waiting.

"Yes." She breathed the word, then reached for him.

He kissed her, and Abby wished she could freeze this moment for all eternity.

Noah pulled away and picked up the ring, holding it out to her. "If you would allow me?" He smiled.

She offered him her hand, and Noah slid the thin band onto her ring finger.

"I love you so much," Abby whispered, leaning in to kiss him, but he gently held her chin before she could.

"Thank you for making me the happiest man in the world. And I promise, you can pick any ring you like. I got this one made for you back when we were in high school and I worked all those odd summer jobs."

She took his hand in his and kissed him.

"I don't want another ring, Noah. This one is perfect."

And when he kissed her again, her heart was full.

Epilogue

Three months later

The cabin buzzed with activity. All six of Noah's brothers had come to Hope Rock for the wedding. His sister was there, too. Of course, Natalie and Brad had brought Edie, their two baby girls, Hailey and Sarah and of course Chip, the rescue puppy. Edie apparently had fallen in love with him, so they'd decided to adopt him themselves.

Of course, Abby and Noah had invited the entire church, including Noah's Sunday school class. The Hope Rock Veterinary Clinic was closed today, as none of Noah's coworkers wanted to miss the wedding.

Standing by the window of her bedroom, her compact in hand, Abby added the finishing touches to her makeup. She looked across the backyard, at the large tent set up to accommodate all their guests. The mountains, their peaks white with fresh snow, provided the perfect backdrop.

She was ready to meet Noah under the white flower canopy, where he would be waiting with their pastor and his groomsmen at his side. Brad had graciously accepted the honor of being his best man.

Charlotte and Edie had talked Abby into letting them dress Rosie and Cinnamon in matching white outfits and to give Briggs a bow tie. Thankfully, Brad had put his foot down and said Chip had to stay in the kennel with the rest of the puppies. Four dogs at the wedding would be a tad too much to handle.

The girls were wearing identical white dresses. Abby smiled as she recalled their excitement when she'd asked them if they would like to be flower girls during the ceremony.

The door to the bedroom opened. Abby looked up, wanting to make sure it wasn't Noah, too impatient to see her.

Charlotte's head poked through the open door. Thinking that no one was looking, she tiptoed toward the closet. Abby watched her reach for the yellow craft case.

"Charlotte, what—"

Her daughter whipped around. Her mouth fell open.

"Wow!" Charlotte almost dropped the yellow case.

Abby smiled. "What do you think?"

"You look…"

And for the first time in her life, Charlotte seemed at a loss for words.

Abby ran her fingers down the long white gown that reached the floor.

"Too much sparkle?" She twirled around so that her daughter could see the back of the dress, too.

The shimmering rhinestones caught the sunlight and cast dazzling reflections across the entire room. As rainbows danced on the walls, Charlotte let go of the yellow case and walked toward Abby, her beautiful blue eyes filling with tears.

"Mommy—" She exhaled. "You look like a fairy princess."

Abby reached for her, and Charlotte buried her face in the delicate lace flowers that cascaded down Abby's sleeves and the right side of her gown. And when her daughter looked up, she smiled through her tears.

"I like your veil. Can I touch it? I don't have glue on my hands, promise."

Abby couldn't help but laugh.

"Of course." She bent down and wrapped her arms around her girl. "I love you so much, sweetheart."

"I love you, too, Mommy," Charlotte whispered against her chest. "Thank you for marrying Noah."

Abby let go of the embrace and looked her daughter in the eyes.

"What? Why would you thank me for that, silly?"

"Because when you marry him, I can hyponate my name."

"You mean hyphenate?"

"Yes. I think Charlotte Clifford-Ross sounds much better than plain Charlotte Clifford."

Abby laughed.

"And here I thought you would say something deep, like, 'thank you for marrying Noah because he is kind and patient and lets me do everything I want to.'"

"Everyone knows that, Mom." Charlotte glanced back at the abandoned craft case. "But you forgot to add the most important thing."

"And what's that?"

"Because he loves me, of course."

Abby hugged her again, willing the tears to stop. She had no time to redo her makeup. Charlotte pulled away and looked at her.

"You may not want to cry, so he doesn't think you don't want to marry him. You know, he loves you, too," she added, then rushed toward the door. She grabbed her craft case. "The flower petals in our baskets need a little bit of glitter. But I can't chat anymore, Mom. Edie and I can't be late. Noah is counting on us. And you should hurry up, too." She carried on excitedly, obviously regaining her gift of gab. "He's already waiting for you under the flower thing."

The door shut and the room fell silent. Abby adjusted her veil. She was so nervous, wanting everything to be perfect. Abby glanced at her ring finger, the Colorado diamond ring shining bright in the afternoon sunlight. It would soon be joined by the heart eternity band, also crafted with rare Colorado diamonds, that Noah had designed for her.

She opened the door and caught Natalie's eye. Her best friend, the matron of honor, cued the music and took her place by the altar. The two flower girls walked in a practiced rhythm down the white carpet, toward the floral canopy, scattering petals and glitter all around them. A hush fell over the room as everyone stood and turned in her direction. Abby filled her lungs and took the first step toward the handsome groom, beaming with love, wearing a tux, his cowboy boots and a fawn-colored Stetson.

For a heartbeat, Abby felt the world narrow to the man waiting at the end of the aisle. The soft rustle of dresses, the faint perfume of roses, the sparkle of petals at her feet—all faded beside the steady warmth in his eyes. Each step carried her closer to the future she had once thought lost, yet now stood radiant and waiting, wrapped in forgiveness, friendship, and the kind of love that could weather every storm.

The glow of the soft rays of the Colorado sun and the shimmer of glitter on the carpet seemed to rise around her like blessings made visible. When she reached him, her heart knew what her lips could not yet speak: this was the beginning of forever, a story only God could have written, stitched together with paw prints, boundless grace, second chances and the unshakable promise of love renewed.

* * * * *

Dear Reader,

Thank you for joining Abby and Noah Ross, little Charlotte, and Rosie and Briggs on their heartwarming journey in *A K-9 Mountain Promise*! It's been a delight to bring their story to life.

As I wrote about the Ross family navigating love, trust and the joys (and occasional chaos!) of raising these wonderful dogs, one truth kept shining through—God walks with us in every season of life. Abby's courage, Noah's patience, Charlotte's innocent joy, and the dogs' boundless loyalty remind us that faith isn't about having everything figured out—it's about trusting God, even when life is messy. I hope this story encourages you to hold onto that unwavering hope in your own journey.

I'd love to hear from you. You can reach me through my website, www.helenasmrcek.com. Thank you for reading and for letting Abby, Noah, Charlotte and the dogs into your heart.

God bless,
Helena Smrcek